QUICK *stories*
by T. M. McNally

University of Michigan Press

Ann Arbor

Copyright © by T. M. McNally 2004
All rights reserved
Published in the United States of America by
The University of Michigan Press
Manufactured in the United States of America
♾ Printed on acid-free paper

2007   2006   2005   2004   4   3   2   1

*A CIP catalog record for this book is available
from the British Library.*

Library of Congress Cataloging-in-Publication Data

McNally, T. M.
    Quick : stories / T.M. McNally.
       p.   cm.
    ISBN 0-472-11452-2 (cloth : alk. paper)
    1. United States—Social life and customs—
Fiction. I. Title.
PS3563.C38816Q53   2004
813'.54—dc22   2004008419

To Matt

This is cactus land

—T. S. Eliot

Contents

One

Muscle (And the Possibility of Grace)

The need for strength is something we understand even then, during our first semester, when life is not yet a matter of avoiding death—the gray wash of despair; a fluke car accident on a long, coastal highway. For us the future is that in which we believe. We are the hopeful, however uninspired. We are Freshmen.

Stilt is screaming. He lies on his back, working the bench, sweating and screaming the way women do during sex. A man will bite his tongue and roll over onto his side, but real women scream: we men here are smart enough to know. Also, it's the kind of thing I dream about at night, looking up at my girlfriend, Susan, who leans against the cinderblock wall just below the window. She is wearing her cotillion dress—white as a wedding, complete with a veil; clearly, she is coming out, and sometimes, looking up, I wonder what she would have sounded like, doing it. I think if we didn't love each other, maybe I would have found out. When she took me to the airport she said she'd love me forever. Her hair smelled like creosote and dust.

But men scream under pressure only. When Stilt screams, lifting the bar, pressing it square over his head, it becomes suddenly clear he doesn't realize the true value of restraint. Except for JD, the transfer student, we—me, Stiltman, Rosco, Mathias—are eighteen each, and Stilt is somehow all of us—wrestling with the bar, struggling for control. In our lives right now, balance is what we require most, and Stilt lies on the bench sweating and screaming. I stand behind him, spotting, and a breeze catches the drapes. It stirs the air in the room. On the wall is a poster of a well-built celebrity describing the hood of a foreign car. The furniture is imitation wood and vinyl, pushed to the side—and looking, I think this is where I live. I think the air smells like vinegar and socks and everything, eventually, is going to make perfect sense.

"I love her," Stilt says, later, flexing into the mirror. "What can I say?"

I'm the one from Phoenix. JD comes from Massachusetts. *The Cape,* we say, because we want to be like him. My psychiatrist has called me angry and manic and periodically threatens me with medication. Weekends is when it gets worse, at night, when the sky begins to really deepen. Sometimes I think it's big enough to die in. Sometimes I think it's responsible for what it overlooks, though I'm not yet mature enough to articulate this, or any other real, idea. I know only that something is growing slowly in my bones, and that when I sleep, I wake up screaming because I can feel it—that feeling, deep in the center of your bones.

"Exercise," says JD. "Exercise is the best thing for sleep."

We are sitting on the roof of Watkins Chapel with a twelve-pack of domestic beer and a fifth of sour mash. Most people are at the Halloween dance, meaning less than half the two hundred and twenty-seven girls living on campus, and we are sitting on the roof looking at the sky. Stilt is eating dinner alone with Mrs. Chamberlain, who is the mother of Charlotte Chamberlain. Charlotte is the girl Stilt loves even though Charlotte is dating a hockey player named Brian O'Malley. When Stilt came by to borrow a pair of black shoes, JD told him he looked *stunning.*

But above us now—me and JD—the sky is full of autumn and ghosts. The wind is growing brisk and JD points out the constellations. He shows me a satellite.

"There," he says, lying back, pointing. "There. That's a satellite, Davey."

Only JD calls me Davey. I pop a beer and think satellites are too high up, they fly too fast—if we were meant to see them, we'd know exactly what they were doing up there.

I say, "Right now, Stiltman is washing dishes. He's washing dishes and telling Mrs. Chamberlain how love truly feels."

JD spits out his beer, it's that funny. He sits up, spreads wide his arms, and howls, "Charlotte! But, but I *love* you!"

Deep down it could be true. JD doesn't say this, but he's the strongest guy on campus and, as we see it, the most deserving of her affections. Charlotte Chamberlain says she's going to try out for the Minnesota Viking cheerleaders; sometimes, she comes over to our room to study with JD because of the way he always knows what's going to be on an exam. When she's not around, people make fun of the way she puts on her jeans, tightly, and while everyone knows she's got a body smooth as porcelain, she's nothing next to Susan. I've seen Susan's body naked, in the back seat of her father's four-wheel drive, during the day. We drove into the middle of the desert with two gallons of water, just to be safe, and when I remember how her body looks, I know that it is real. I know that it is real and meaningful and just waiting for me to come home from some college stuck in the middle of Minnesota.

JD knows how it is. That's why we're on the roof of Watkins Chapel avoiding all the lonely girls on campus. The muscles in my back are full of knots, and when he passes me the whiskey, I think even pain will make a body feel good.

No pain, no gain: the January term lasts a month, in between semesters, where you take one class and spend a lot of time looking for something else to do. For example, I am learning how to build a dulcimer from scratch, and where I'm from, it never snows. During my Christmas break, I went home, and Susan and I went skinny-dipping in a pool . . . one night, almost, but we didn't have *protection,* and already now my Christmas tan has faded. When I say words with *O*s in them, people think I'm local.

In Minnesota, the snow is deep and on national TV. At night it gets so cold I begin to understand what it means to feel lonely, here, in Minnesota, where the sun has died and turned to ice. And stumbling out of the Blue Ox with Stilt and JD and Rosco and Mathias, stumbling, I'm beginning to think all this is pretty funny—last call, and closing time. "That was a last call," I say, but no one seems to notice. Inside the bar was a girl I thought I'd like to try and talk to. The girl had skin the color of snow. For some reason, I am discovering, I become less shy when it is really cold.

"Charlotte!" yells Rosco. "But Charlotte!"

"I can't help it," says Stilt.

"You know," says Mathias, "I heard she does it with a flashlight."

When I pick on Stilt, it makes me not mind being with him. Last week, Stilt wrote Charlotte a long letter, explaining he just didn't think it was going to work out, that being in love and loving another being just weren't the same thing. The next day Brian O'Malley, the hockey star, who was also a DJ for the college radio, read Stilt's letter over the air; the station is wired into the cafeteria during breakfast and lunch so people can listen in. He read Stilt's entire letter during lunch and then played a special song just for those experiencing *unrequested love.* While he was reading, you could hear people chewing their food, and all night long Stilt's been saying he's humiliated. Also, we've been drinking imports.

"And this one's going out to the Stiltman," said Brian O'Malley, just before putting on the song.

And now in the parking lot on a Friday night where Stilt's feeling terribly misunderstood and drunk, after *Last Call,*

Rosco is trying to pick somebody up. The girl is trying to make her car go but the wheels keep spinning on the ice. "Hey," Rosco says. "Hey!"

"Best letter I ever helped write," I say.

"I thought it was beautiful," says JD.

Rosco is still talking to the girl, and inside the car is a fat guy big as the moon, and now the fat guy's yelling at Rosco. He's getting out of the car, taking off his jacket.

"Hey," says JD, waving. "Just having a good time."

"Really," I say to the fat guy. "That was a really last call."

It's cold, too, so cold my jacket makes noises when I move. I think the fat guy says something stupid and lots of people are starting to pay attention, including a group of guys who seem to know him. The fat guy's feeling big, pushing me around, and JD says, "Hey. Hey!"

By now there's lots of names going back and forth and I'm thinking this is something I'm going to want to remember. JD and me, I think. Me and JD—we're going to kick some God damn ass, and I'm saying things now, just waiting, and JD, too, and the fat guy's friends, the snow's about to fly, and me and JD, we're in the center. We're in the center of it all.

"Nobody lives forever," I say, which I have always understood to be true.

Two weeks later, me and JD are in court, defending ourselves, and it still hurts when I sneeze. My eyes are swollen with dark, bloody rings, and the judge is looking at his watch. It's been a busy day. He's explaining the need for self-control and community service. My father's lawyer wires me money to pay the fine, and now, after we finish working out, we drive in JD's big car downtown to play basketball with the poor kids. We pass the ball back and forth to the kids and blow whistles: JD in his sweats, waving his hands, yelling. Eventually, Stilt drops out, because he's been publicly humiliated by a guy named Brian O'Malley, and Susan's mother, Joyce, calls me from Phoenix. On the phone she explains that my father is in the hospital and that she thinks it would be a good idea if I came home soon as possible.

"Okay," I say, talking to her on the phone. "How's Susan?"

I learn things slowly. What happened, too, is enough to shake your faith in love. My father saw Susan driving around town with another guy and called her a whore. He called her a whore on the doorstep of her dormitory, and then he tried to throttle her. After he ripped open her blouse, she kicked him, hard, and he went down and vomited. Then the police came by and carried him away.

And it's possible to realize the moment in greater detail— the city night air, full of car exhaust and traffic lights, pretty people strolling by in fine cotton sweaters, the big glass doors leading in to Manzanita Hall; my father, still in his suit, his tie undone and full of stains because he's stopped taking his lithium, and the booze—but these are details I don't pursue for fear of understanding too clearly who I am. Meanwhile, I fly into Sky Harbor and rent my very first car; I drive to the Superstition Mountain Care Facility, a place I've been to often. There my father sits in a garden wearing Bermuda shorts, drinking a Coke, smiling. He's talking to a woman with long black hair. The woman's eyes are full of humiliation and disease, like my father's, and what I want to know, right now, right now as I'm standing here in the sunshine staring at my father, is just what the hell he expects me to do now?

"I was protecting your God damn honor," he says. "How's school?"

Behind him, the woman is looking away at a lemon tree, listening.

"Thanks," I say, referring to his last check.

He shrugs. "So things are okay, then. Yeah?"

"Yeah," I say. "Okay."

And now my father is in tears, blinking. "I thought she might have heard from you, all right? I was thinking maybe she might know something!"

He's screaming at me now, taking a swing, the woman is walking slowly away, trying not to appear dangerous or alarmed. She walks slowly away from range while the security guards with tennis clothes and shaved heads are jogging across the lawn—and here I am, still standing.

Two days later I'm visiting Susan at the state university, and what I'm thinking is that the building she lives in is tall as anything in Minneapolis. Her roommate is wearing a tank top without a bra getting ready for a date. The walls are full of horses and men on skis, a seagull flying into the sky. Susan sits on her bed in khaki shorts and a sweatshirt, saying things about her classes. When I ask her questions about what happened, she waves her hand and smiles: apparently, some things no longer matter.

"So," she says, leaning back on her hands. "Do you want to go to a party?"

We go, and at the party are people in fraternities. They drink beer like anybody else but seem uncertain of what to do with people who don't look quite like them. Simply, my hair is too long, my skin pale from wintering in the great north woods, and my date has been sleeping with the treasurer of Alpha Tau Omega. Troy says, holding his stein in one hand, a clove cigarette in the other, nice things to me about Susan, and you can tell by the way their eyes meet they're feeling sorry for me—the little guy with feelings nobody really wants to hurt. I think if I wanted to, I could break this guy's neck: one hand there, on the clavicle, another up against his jaw; maybe I'd smile real big and twist. I think this guy is someday going to get what he deserves, maybe even Susan, and now I look at her and say, "I'm sorry, but I've got to go."

When I get home, I pour myself a water-glass full of gin and call long distance. I sit on the kitchen floor and tell JD he doesn't know what he's missing. Here, in Arizona, where it's eighty-five degrees. I tell him he's missing lots, not being here. I tell him I don't think I'm the kind of guy you should have a family with.

But faith is a right we need to exercise, to keep it strong, and while I forgive my father, I want at the same time to be capable of doing otherwise. Meanwhile, I tell him I'll write, and when I leave Susan shows up at the airport. Outside the terminal, standing by a cab, she says, "I'm sorry. You know I'm really sorry."

Things change, she says. She is wearing a peach dress, and this is the last time I ever talk to her. As for my father, he dries out, for good this time, and eventually decides to retire in five years to sail the Caribbean: it's a place neither of us has ever been before. We don't even know how to sail. On the phone he asks me if I want to come along, and I say, "Yeah. Sure."

"It's something your mother would have wanted us to do," he says, which is always dangerous—when he starts talking about my mother, his dead wife, and now that I'm back at school, in my English class, I think things are going to get worse. I think my heart no longer works properly, that's why I feel so bad: this, in the center of my chest, the slow burn of loss. When Stilt comes up to visit for *Spring Fling*, he asks me how's it going.

"Okay," I say. "I've moved up on the bench."

"Squats?"

"Yeah," I say. "Squats too."

And now I sit on my heels, outside where the air is wet, the grass green. Watching the grass grow, I think this is why poets pay so much attention to spring: because it hurts. In our room alone we have two kegs of beer and fruit punch laced with Everclear.

"How's Susan?" Stilt asks, meaning he wants to talk about Charlotte Chamberlain. I stand, stretching my calves, wondering why it is he can't tell I'm different. I take him into our room, and on the way he says, "It's true, you know. That part about the flashlight."

Inside it's full of pale bodies and sweat and the sweet, stale smell of beer: it really is spring, and even the people here are wearing t-shirts and shorts. In Arizona, the saguaros are preparing to bloom, and Stilt, he's working at a department store in Duluth, *Men's Wear,* living with his mother and thinking about the Coast Guard. My mother died when I was thirteen, and Stilt says he gets his clothes now at a discount. JD laughs at that, because he thinks Stilt dresses like a pimp.

"Charlotte," JD yells. "But I *love* you!"

By now JD is pretty drunk. He's wearing his pink muscle shirt and you can see the stretch marks shooting under his arms. Now he's pretending to play the violin. The music is loud, Connie Fitzgerald is dancing on top of a desk, Stilt is spilling out his chest, posing, and now JD looks up at me, smiling, playing the violin.

Later, the phone rings, and it's for me, and Rosco turns down the stereo. I take the phone into the bathroom, where there's a keg in the shower and everybody's muddy shoes; outside people are trying to be quiet, which is impossible, and on the phone I talk to my father's secretary, Shirley Dunnaway, who's explaining all the way from Phoenix, Arizona, just what's happened and where the body is. When I hang up, I go outside and sit on the steps. The lawns are wet and full of mud; by dark you'll never know spring was ever here, and eventually, it's likely even your lungs will freeze.

"Davey," says JD, stumbling up behind me. "Davey, what's going on?"

During exams it's easy to pretend you know the answers, and I'm thinking that this is going to take some getting used to and that probably I'm going to fail. I'm going to get washed out, like Stilt, and no one, not even my father, is ever going to know why, and now JD sits on the steps beside me. He puts his arm around my shoulder and says, "Well, was she worth it?"

Rowing builds the lats; running slows your heart rate; self-pity atrophies the soul. My father's liver was swollen with loss, and if you stand in the mirror long enough, you begin to see what you really look like. If he hadn't killed himself, I think, maybe he wouldn't have wanted to.

Still, and eventually, time passes—a couple summers in Taos, vacations in Mazatlan, but for the next three years I keep returning here where my life keeps going on. JD and I are no longer roommates because I have a girlfriend now. Oddly enough, her name is also Susan, and she represents neither my first nor my last conjugal experience, though each time of course I think it's both. I have learned, too, at least here in a college with thin walls, that it is best to stifle the particular noises you and your girlfriend might equally be inclined to make. Mornings, when Susan leaves my room, she sneaks out through the window.

Simply, we have rules to follow, and love, like the body, requires constant definition: my girlfriend takes the pill and perms her hair. Her shampoo smells like oranges, and she is a local girl studying Economics. At home, she has a hope chest, and an organ which will replicate the sound of a drum and any number of horns. Her parents invite me often for dinner and, to my surprise, seem to like me. Her father manages a shoe store downtown; he is very proud of his little girl. "Cute as a button," he'll say, passing me a Coke. "Cute as a God damn button!"

And my girlfriend says she wants to marry me. She wants to marry me and move into an apartment while I finish my degree, and one night, while she is taking off her sweater, I look up at her body and wonder. Her body is strong from doing aerobics, which are just now beginning to be popular: her arms and shoulders are full of unexpected muscles. She has moles in places you wouldn't think there should be any, and they look nice—these small, dark passages in her skin. Naked, she looks younger than she really is.

"I love you, Dave," she says.

It's what she always says, and I feel unexpectedly mature and forthright. Too, if I don't say anything, I know what she's going to do next: we've been together long enough to develop rhythm, and I know she's looking at my body the way I'm looking at hers. I know that blood requires oxygen to breathe, that the heart is a muscle big as your fist, that love is something you have to believe in first.

Now she has her hand on my chest, and I look up at her. I breathe in slow and say, "Hey, maybe we oughta call it quits?"

My advisor calls me *The Orphan*. He is a thin man who speaks five languages and jogs in between his classes. During the days, you see him running through the campus, swinging his arms into propellers; if he gets up enough speed, he just might someday take off. He is a man whose strength relies on flexibility, and when I ask him questions about seminary, he tells me to go to law school. "Grow rich," he tells me. "Become a pillar of the church." But this an answer I'm not looking for.

Whenever I ask JD what I should do, he always says, "Well, what do you want to do?"

JD knows my secret, and so he knows already that we both know what I am going to try and do with my life. It's the type of conversation we have late at night, and one night, in JD's room, whiskey and beer, he tells me a story from last semester. Apparently, JD is up on the seventh floor of the vault with Charlotte Chamberlain. She never made the cheerleading squad and has recently decided to finish her degree in Education, later she will become a flight attendant for a failing airline, but right now she is with JD and it is three, maybe four o'clock in the morning when the phone rings. Charlotte answers, thinking maybe it's her mother in Paris, or Brian O'Malley, melancholic and drunk, but there's no one on the other end. JD says to me, laughing, reaching for a beer, "A prank call!"

When he says that word, *call,* it's easy to trace the place of his origins—Massachusetts. He lights a cigar, points to the bottle, which I accept, and JD keeps going on: thus, and so inclined, they curl back in the sack which is still remarkably warm, but he has this feeling, this really pleasant feeling that someone he knows is watching over him. He feels something going on but okay about it all, too, *you know?* and then the fire alarm goes off. The fire alarm is loud enough to freeze your brain. JD, he's running around looking for his pants, and then the doors start opening and closing, opening and closing: the dormitory needs to be evacuated, the RAs are going through the halls, and aside from the rules, no one is supposed to know JD and Charlotte Chamberlain are getting it on behind Brian O'Malley's back, anyway—and now he's in Charlotte's pink and green bathrobe, going down the stairs, surrounded by girls who know, and Rosco, whom JD meets up with on the fifth floor. The girls swirl all around Rosco and JD and keep them going down the stairs until, outside, barefoot in the snow, JD looks up at the seventh floor. There in Charlotte's room, there behind the lit glass of her room, is Brian O'Malley, jacking off.

JD looks at the cigar in his hand. He reaches for the bottle and says, "I never told anyone." Now he's closing his eyes, shaking his head, his hands nearly full. "Anyone."

It's something I never knew. When I told my girlfriend I thought maybe we should call it quits, she stood up on the bed and kicked me in the ribs. Then she started punching me, her fists knotted up, punching away. She pulled my hair and screamed. Once she started screaming, she stopped punching, and eventually she put on her clothes.

I walked her out to her car, wearing only my boots and jeans, a t-shirt; I stood by her car and shivered in the snow.

Then I got in and she began to drive. She drove for hours, down streets I'd never been before, never saying a word. Once we skidded on some ice, but she was good at driving, she knew always where she wanted to end up: with a house, and decent people inside who needed her. Finally, she drove me back to campus, put the car into neutral, and kissed me. She kissed me the way she did before she knew me, and then she drove away to Washington, DC, where she married a pathologist. But back then I didn't know she was going to be happy for the rest of her life. I thought she was going to do something stupid. I thought about Susan, wearing her peach dress, climbing into a cab.

Once I picked a fight with Brian O'Malley. A party, outside, the keg stuffed in the snow. I wanted to see if he could do it.

"Give it up," he said.

And clearly this guy was beyond my reach. He played hockey, he was used to fighting with sticks; he had arms long as trees. When it was over, JD took a wad of snow and held it up against my cheek. He poured me a fresh beer and said, "Now why did you do that?"

And then Charlotte Chamberlain drifted over, carrying a flashlight and wading through the snow, her boots up to her knees. She put her arm around my shoulder and asked me if I was okay; even outside with her parka on, you could smell her perfume. She smelled like a department store.

JD says that's when things started happening: that night with me and the split cheek—and Charlotte and JD, putting me quietly to bed, adjusting the knobs on the stereo, closing the door and walking off together down the hallway. And just four months before graduation, when Brian O'Malley drives his car through a doughnut shop window on Sixth Avenue, we suspect there's alcohol in his bloodstream. At the memorial service in Watkins Chapel the visitors are timid and pale. Charlotte Chamberlain gives a moving, if somewhat digressive, eulogy, and Stilt, who drives in from

Duluth just to see the show, says he understands how it must have felt.

And all the while I'm thinking about my father. People are moving to the reception area, crying, telling jokes, heading for the beer, and now my advisor arrives late. He's wearing his sweats, and I understand for the first time in my life what my father must have always known to be possible. Home, where I'm still only thirteen—I'm thinking about my father sitting by the poolside. He sits by the pool, sipping iced coffee, and he tells me to sit down.

"Your mom," he says, sitting in the sun. "Your mom's not as strong as she used to be."

Inside the house, she's wearing her blue swimsuit, the one that covers her stretch marks but still shows off her hips. She's lying on the top of the couch, resting.

"You must be strong, David."

"Okay," I say, and then I grow up. I learn to change the spark plugs in my car and write an essay, fix TV dinners, go to prom. I learn to shake hands with important people and be polite. My girlfriend's name was Susan. Later, Brian O'Malley fell in love with Charlotte Chamberlain, and here at the memorial service held in honor of the dead, and everyone else I'm ever going to know, I am watching JD. He is standing up against the wall. He is standing up against the wall wearing the tweed coat his mother picked out, which no longer fits, and I'm thinking if he wants to, he can raise the entire building. I'm thinking love may very well be what the body longs for, but it feeds on muscle.

The last time I saw JD, I don't remember what he said. I don't even remember where I was. There was a time there that is gone now—years worth, years spent all across the country, trying to pay attention and survive. I do remember that we didn't talk as much as we should have, that there were things I should have told him. I'm told he caught a plane a couple years later for Florida, where he was going to meet up with his parents and do some deep sea fishing. And sometimes now I imagine him, sitting on a cramped plane, eating his peanuts. Maybe Charlotte Chamberlain, now in her flight uniform, carrying a tray of drinks—maybe Charlotte Chamberlain comes strolling down the aisle. Maybe they talk about people they used to know, plan to meet up sometime along the beach for dinner. Probably, there's a little turbulence, because history is a weight you have to get used to: where you come from; or someone you used to know, lying dead on a coastal highway, his face full of broken glass.

But I don't think death is half as tough as learning to ski, or reading the right books, or making love with your wife. We live in Jerome, which sits right on top of Mingus Mountain; we spend a lot of time outside taking hikes. We have a town center and tourists and just enough snow in winter to make the scenery pretty, and each morning, before I lift, I look out at the sky. Here the weather changes often, but you can see it when it does: there, off in the distance, with the clouds spilling over the Mogollon Rim. Sooner or later, you know they're going to come home; you can see the weather coming from miles off and you know it's going to snow and that after, before it all melts, before you even have time to start a pot of coffee, you know you're going to understand that something's happened. Something meaningful enough to change the way you want to live. That snow, and the life you're going to try and follow, forthwith.

Recovery

Meanwhile I walked home from school alone, my dress torn, my underwear tucked inside my bookbag. I wanted to take the car, go to the store, maybe do some shopping, but this was 1979—a recession clearly in the works, another cycle of economic speculation leading to inexplicable despair. The car needed a new set of tires and a brake job. My father would let me drive it only on Sundays, to take us all to church, or to go shopping for food and drink, but not for clothes. I hadn't bought clothes in nearly two years, not since May left to become rich and famous in New York City. Usually, I stole, and walking home I thought I'd like to get myself a pair of purple shoes, to go with a sweater I used to have. In the fall, at the first sign of brisk weather, I'd put on my sweater and admire the way it caught the light; I liked the way the wool felt against my skin, reminding me that it was my skin, and that it was capable of feeling something simple as a pretty sweater on a brisk, sunny day: I went through the gate leading into the backyard, and the swimming pool, thinking about a sweater I used to have. Jimmy was sitting on the diving board over the swimming pool, throwing rocks, and inside the house Daddy sat naked in the living room. He was looking at the picture of May in a catalogue, the part for women's underwear.

"It's good to see you," he said.

"Sorry I'm late."

"Come here."

"Jimmy," I said. "He's outside. He's filling up the swimming pool."

"What did you do to your dress? Come over here. Come over here now and let me have a look at you."

"No," I said.

Instead I sat on his lap, which pleased him momentarily. He was too drunk to find a way inside. When he began to weep, I got up to fix us dinner. Noodles and Tab. I called Jimmy into the house and asked him to find us light bulbs; I promised to take him out for ice cream if he helped me clean the kitchen. Jimmy wouldn't eat. At the table, my father explained to us the value of hard work and discipline. Then he sent me to the store for a bottle of blended Scotch. He said there were a couple of fives in the car, beneath the floor mat; he praised my cooking and, when Jimmy began to fidget, slapped him silly.

"Come on, Jimmy," I said, taking his hand. "Come with."

The clock sits on an ottoman beside a plant where we both can see it clearly. My lover once said I am a cynic, and what I could not tell him is what I know to be true: to explain the roots of my experience would be to challenge his expectations for a safe and happy life. I have since learned that cynicism and despair are mutually exclusive. One can only expect the worst if one knows what might in fact or deed be better. Cynicism assumes that things will always fail to measure up, but still we have a device with which to measure their ascent; the cynic always has the potential to hope for a better way of life—the possibility for change, which for the desperate remains always far removed. I tell myself cynicism at its best is a form of false modesty. I say to everything there is a season; even in the 1930s, people still hoped for change: standing in line, longing for a piece of bread, a raw lump of rancid beef. My father was born into the great depression, like a number of other well-intentioned boys, and somehow, somehow along the way he decided to serve his country and to try and hold a job and to marry my mother, and when she finally left, with a blackened eye and several cracked ribs, we stayed behind, waiting—for Jimmy to try and learn to speak; or for May to send us plane tickets. And when nothing happened, nothing happened. My father continued to sit unemployed inside the living room. Jimmy turned silent as the flesh. And I . . . I rearranged my dress and told boys at school how much I really wanted to change the world.

"Okay," Evangalene says, smiling. "Okay. When did things start to get out of hand?"

You see the truly desperate are the eternally damned. I took Jimmy's hand and led him outside. My father was mistaken: beneath the floor mat, beside the car keys, there was almost fifty dollars, and seeing that much money, the most money I had ever seen in one place that actually belonged to my daddy, I thought of the swimming pool. Daddy could buy some chlorine and fill the pool. Or he could order himself a mail-order suit, maybe a newspaper subscription. He could ask me to drive him downtown in order to renew his driver's license, which had been expired for years, and then he could find a job, a job he could in fact hold onto: I'd help him get up in the mornings, fix him breakfast, maybe make his bed. Thus, I held the money in my hand while Jimmy rolled down the window, and then I started up the car. Gas was going up in price back then. The car started unexpectedly and I backed out of the drive, slowly, the way I always did, and when I reached the end of our street, I told Jimmy to fasten his seatbelt.

I didn't have instructions to Mom's house. I didn't even know where she lived. May lived in New York City, which was all the way across the country, and I was nervous about driving in too much traffic. I stopped at the high school and found a screwdriver beneath the seat and exchanged license plates with a dusty pickup. Across the parking lot was the girl's restroom, and the lockers; I went to my locker and removed my books, my windbreaker, three packs of chewing gum and a box of Trojans. I cleaned it out and wanted to leave a note, but I couldn't think of what to say, and so instead I left a sheet of notebook paper. The paper was purple and had thin lines, the way I liked them, and on the floor, in the dark corner, you could see the condoms my boyfriend and his dealer, Tully Crenshaw, had used just a few hours ago. My boyfriend had bet Tully Crenshaw he couldn't last seven minutes.

"Seven," my boyfriend said. "I bet you can't go seven minutes."

Tully was shy in front of my boyfriend. He was used to privacy and upholstered car seats. Normally, you could fog up the windows easily.

"Wait," I said, sliding out of my underwear.

"If you do it," my boyfriend said, "you can't tell anybody."

"What if she gets pregnant?"

"She won't tell anybody, either," said my boyfriend. And then, turning to me, winking, he said, "Will you, June?"

I was raised to believe in secrets. I didn't use condoms to avoid pregnancy; I used condoms to prevent my father's knowing. Once, when I had an affair, I returned to condoms for the same purpose: to keep my lover, the man who calls me a cynic, from incidentally discovering my infidelity. I slept with another man because I wanted to leave my lover but was afraid to. I love the man who calls me a cynic, but I know too that eventually we must destroy each other, which is why he has since left me for his ex-wife. To marry would be to make holy the ties which bind us, most of which are knotted up into my past. I learned at a very young age I cannot endure the weight of man.

Jimmy was always silent. The night Mom left, she said she was going to the liquor store; she asked if we'd like a candy bar, maybe some soda pop? Her eye was swollen shut and when she coughed she held her side. The ribs are sensitive, the way they curve—a cage God made to keep the vital organs safe: the heart, the liver and lungs. Jimmy and I sat outside on the porch, waiting, and even then we knew she wasn't going to return. There had been too much damage done. Mornings, she had begun to cough up blood.

And I've heard stories. I know some women forget for years what's been done to their bodies—a random uncle, sneaking in to visit; a sentimental step-daddy, occasionally drunk and caught off-guard. These women wait for years before, some early morning, with birds outside, chirping, they wake up and realize they've been violated. Meanwhile they have to learn to survive all over again, though if they only asked themselves, they'd know that's what they already know how to do better than anybody could have ever taught them. And let me tell you, I always knew. I always knew, and I promised not to tell, because I always knew it was my fault: my daddy did not have to fuck me, and had I never been born, it never would have been. To survive, one must first learn the rules, and such reasoning keeps us dangerously alive. We learn not to be afraid of blood. We learn it is easier to die than it is to live.

Meanwhile, I am taking Tofrinal now, 150 mgs a day, and still I know it is no good. I know that I am dying. I know that grief will smother even a mother's heartbeat, and I know if it were not for grief, I could have saved myself from this need for medication, and sleep, and always, always the center of the night.

"June," my daddy used to say, before Mom left for liquor and treats. "June is busting out all over."

Sometimes, he'd ask me to sing, and I never forgot. I have never let it go.

Today I learned that the United States destroys weekly billions of gallons of milk. Hunger, it would seem, is merely the result of inadequate distribution, and now, having moved into another city, looking back on my life from yet another region, I still have a picture of Hillary and Bill on my refrigerator. They are standing on a platform in Daley Square, surrounded by a crowd of Democrats. Somewhere, I know, I am standing there among them, and it is a hopeful scene, one describing a candid moment by way of a telephoto lens: even up close, Hillary and Bill are beautiful. Clearly, they are in love with each other and what they just might yet accomplish—victory, and the still unblemished possibility for hope. Hillary is wearing a plum-colored dress, the campaign has hit its second wind, and as for the grieving process, it is variable and indiscriminate, like crime on our city streets. What goes on inside our households often is a shame, and shame, I now know, is what binds us to our past. It's what makes us each complicitous and capable of more: I did not have to do the things that I have done. I did not have to send my lover to New York City and his ex-wife. I did not have to buy a leather sofa. I did not have to celebrate the good times and, in so doing, forget just where I really came from. Yuma, Arizona, which is nothing more than a corporately owned grocery store in the middle of the desert.

But you see as I am explaining this, I am strong again, and Hillary Rodham and Bill are here upon my refrigerator, gently waving in a sea of public affirmation. A vision of the future, possibly: first weeks, then months, then my life begins to pass, and for the most part, you can say that things, like the popular vote, will always turn out in the end, regardless of our common histories. Jimmy went to New York City and, unlike May, caught a disease; he died stepping into a cab off Fifty-seventh Street, carrying the virus and spilling it out onto the pavement. I was in grad school in California when it happened. A man called me up from a pay phone and asked me who I was. May was in Europe at the time with an architect from Brazil. Jimmy had been living with her, floating in and out of NYU and dangerous love affairs, bartending at a place called Tooth & Nail. It took years of counseling before he ever began to speak, in Louisville, because once the police caught up with us, they weren't about to let us live in Hollywood. We were driving stolen property, said the cop. He asked us when was the last time we ate anything.

I said, "We're not very hungry, Mister."

And foster care isn't as bad as most people make it out to be. It's easier to live with strangers than it is with someone you've been raised to love—family values have a tendency to depreciate over time and too much familiarity. Our foster parents gave us pocket money and sent Jimmy to special doctors; they paid for my abortion and encouraged me to take calculus, and fine art, and when it came time for me to go off to college, they told me this was going to be my fresh start; they said I should be certain to do whatever it was I wanted. I could become a concert pianist, or a librarian, or a nurse. I slept with my lover the first time in grad school, before he was married; we met at a famous school and moved in together the way most people who are afraid of following too closely in the steps of their fathers, and mothers, usually do. We lived like normal people who share living quarters briefly and a bed: we ate pasta on weekends; later, he married someone else, then divorced; eventually we bought together expensive cars. We moved to the Windy City and lived nearby the lake. Sunday morning, driving past me, you'd never know my brother had died alone on a street in New York City. To be sure, you'd never know just where I came from.

Once, I went to a career counselor, and he told me the most important thing in life was to learn to sell yourself. Evangalene says the medication will help and tells me not to feel ashamed. She says, spreading out her fingers, there will be a window-pane effect. The dizziness will go away. After a while, maybe we will have a breakthrough?

Recovery, I think. But from what to what? I admire Barbara Jordan deeply, but if you cut the national debt, we'd certainly have a lot more cash to circulate. After all the zeros, the interest begins to add up. If you sleep with strangers, you will bring home precisely what they give you; if you do not pay your bills, you cannot invest into the future. Fortunately, Evangalene is not too big on the dance with anger, and this is the kind of thing Evangalene likes to tell me, though of course she knows I already understand the principles of sound investment. Sometimes, she even asks for pointers. Still, she wants to use a metaphor I might appreciate, and the medication, which makes me dizzy and weak. I no longer drive or get dressed up, and if I drink coffee, I feel as if I'm going to cry. For days, I mean. Once it starts, I'm not likely to stop for days, and I'm discovering other odd and interesting things about myself: things most people wouldn't want to know about anybody, especially those with whom they might engage in cautious conversation—at the grocery store, say, or Marshall Field's. I'm thinking that I've spent years figuring out what was wrong with me only to learn that it wasn't me. It wasn't my fault. *It's not your fault,* Evangalene says, though maybe she just wants to seduce me. *You got kicked around as a kid, it's only normal* . . . and I think even if she did, it wouldn't be all that difficult. One day I walk into a highly recommended psychiatrist's office, and the next I'm pumped full of anti-depressants and, in effect, exonerated. It's time for me to learn to do things I have never done before. Evangalene says the past does not own you. *You have to free yourself from what has happened.*

But what happens next? I mean, you cut away your past, and what does a body have left to stand on? What I mean, Evangalene, is just who is left to tell me who I am?

Right, she says, smiling. There's the rub.

Sometimes I imagine Jimmy, sitting alone in a bar, Tooth

& Nail, picking at his scars. Once he hit fifteen, the acne was contagious; it spread all over his body, despite the medication funded by kind and caring foster parents. By the time he was twenty, I was in grad school, and the sores were finally beginning to look as if they might someday heal, and sometimes I see him, sitting alone, drinking at a bar. Maybe a tall stranger wanders up to him, rests a friendly hand on Jimmy's thigh? Maybe they step into a room to talk, to have sex, to spread the risk of intimacy. You don't need AIDS to illustrate the volatile nature of love, but it does help to inform the general public. Health care is a booming industry, and sometimes I imagine Jimmy, on his knees, taking some strange man or woman by the mouth. Then I think of him all alone, afterwards, and the sweet bitter taste of regret. *It is not the body,* he will write to me. *It is the stranger within. It is always, always the unknown.*

Evangalene doesn't know the half of it, and still she knows it's bad. My lover, who leads a social life, has encouraged me often to invite Evangalene out to dinner. "A conversational threesome, June. I mean, what do you guys talk about?"

"Girl talk," I say.

Then my lover says if things do not change pretty quick, as in October, he is going to move to New York City. He can make twice the money there, he says. He's given our relationship too many years already.

"Time to cut your losses, yeah?"

"June," he says. "Look at you? You can't even leave the house anymore."

He's right, of course. On Tuesdays and Thursdays, I take the El into the city, then a cab to cross the river; since the Michigan Avenue Bridge fell in, the traffic has become complex. Then I take an elevator seventeen flights up to Evangalene's office. Evangalene has suggested perhaps a facility? Just for a couple weeks, to see how it feels.

Precisely, I feel as if I'm dying. Simply I am dying, and I am a thirty-one-year-old woman with a decent man and a lot of money in the bank: I have a stuffed cat, and a leather sofa, and a garage to park my foreign car in. I have a man who loves me more than his ex-wife.

"Go," I say to him. "Cut your losses. Cut cut cut!"

I am holding up the smallest kitchen knife we own, but still it's sharp. I take the knife and draw a line into the back of my wrist. I draw the line up to the elbow, slowly, because things done deliberately often take time. When I am finished, I clean the blade with my tongue. "If you leave me," I say to him, "I won't go any more crazy than I already am."

"You're going to kill yourself," he says. "And I'm not going to watch." He is reaching for a dishtowel for my arm, and now he is wrapping my arm, holding it above my head, as in *first aid,* and I know that I am dying.

"I hate you," I say.

"Shhh," he says.

"Oh God," I say. "Go to hell."

I think of Ben Franklin and James Madison and Alexander Hamilton, who invented the National Debt; I think of Aaron Burr; and Teddy Roosevelt, cruising around in the Great White Fleet; and Henry Adams, discovering for us all that governing principle of energy by which a republic must drive its ships and tanks into the future. And then I think of George Herbert Walker Bush invading Panama, and then Kuwait, each in the spirit of Liberation, as if such a thing were possible for anyone. Quite frankly, we are a nation indebted to more than just our fellow debtors: there is such a thing as history and the resources we have at hand to shape it. When we say it's time for change, all we really mean is that maybe we will have a little loose to give the homeless.

I no longer had much riding on the future of the German mark, either. The yen was plummeting, because now it was time for real change across the corners of the globe. Substantive. Dollars and legislative bills. It was time we looked things in the eye and put our people first. Actually, I wrote Hillary an anonymous letter. *Your husband may be right,* I wrote. *But you should tell him not to smile so much.*

We all know Clinton was raised in a place called Hope. In six weeks I have lost another fifteen pounds, though Evangalene claims I have a heavy heart. October has long since passed, my lover is long and gone, and often now I find myself explaining things to him. Maybe I am simply hoping he will not come back to me again.

"I was mad," I say, looking at my wrist.

Evangalene tilts her face, quizzically, and even I know this is not enough. "Not *mad* mad. I was angry at him for being fine. Every time I look at him, I know that he is fine and it makes me feel as if I'm going to die."

"So you lost your temper?" Evangalene says.

"No," I say. "I lost my head, and now I can't find it, and then I lost my man."

I am weeping now, alone in my chair beside myself without a tree in sight—just a small, potted plant. Evangalene no longer bothers to take any notes; she knows me that well, she thinks. She knows that I am weeping, and ridiculous, and she knows precisely what is wrong with me, though of course she only knows the half of it.

"It's going to take some time," she says, looking at the clock, which always sits between us.

Go ahead, I'm thinking. Fire away, but be careful of the questions you want to ask. Just what do you really need to know? I mean, does my lover really want to know the things I have written about him in my journal? And does he really want to know why I hate his ex-wife? That smug good little woman with the turned-up mouth? And does that little woman really want to know the things that he has said to me?

When he comes, he often calls me bitch, I write. According to Evangalene, it is important I record my thoughts and dreams. By dreams she does not mean ideas I have for tomorrow, like Martin Luther King, or Gandhi. Still, it has been a while; the streets are icy and full of holiday cheer; now when my lover comes, he must always come without me. *I will no longer sleep with a man I am in love with,* I write. It is something new I have also learned about myself.

And later, inside our office, I have decided to bring Evangalene another plant. It is small and slightly decorous, and I am feeling increasingly belligerent.

"So tell me, Evangalene," I say. "Shall I tell his wife? His intended? Whatever the hell she is? I mean, shall I call her up and say, Dear Ex-wife, please know your man no longer has the opportunity to call me bitch?"

"Stop," Evangalene says.

"Stop," I say.

"Unless you're going to follow through. It's fine to beat up on yourself if you take yourself to the hospital, after."

"You mean check myself in?"

She is a smart woman who smiles at me. "No. I mean, if you're going to be mean, you also have to be nice. You're going to have to have it both ways, June."

I lift my arm and smile. "It didn't need any stitches, you know. I'm not crazy. Merely dramatic."

She smiles, accordingly.

"I know you know that," I say. "Now you know that I know that, too."

Because I am almost feeling better, I no longer write the check inside her office: the silence while we wait to fill in all the blanks is too unbearable, and I am discovering that I no longer wish to feel this way. Instead, I bring the check along beforehand, already filled out, complete, and slip it beneath the blotter on the desk on my way out. Stepping outside the building, onto the Miracle Mile with half a million other people, I realize that soon it's going to snow. Nothing, I have always believed, ever makes us special.

Because it's all been done before. We've had Democrats in office more than once. A long time ago, a few fat men gathered together and decided to corner the silver market, and instead they threw the country into an unexpectedly deep depression. You see I'm not the only girl to get shafted by her daddy. To drink too much when she is lonely. To miss my brother because he's dead.

I missed my brother when he was living, like most of us. After all, he didn't like to speak; he sat in school and drew things on the desktop. Our foster parents bought us gifts at Christmas. They taught us how to drive their cars, each with a manual transmission, legally. They encouraged us to bring home friends from school, and I began to date a boy who was a Christian. One Easter, May flew all the way from New York City.

Evangalene doesn't know the half of it, and I am just beginning to recall even more, each day a little bit more clearly. I recall the way my father wanted me to dance with him beneath the carport. The way my mother slept alone at night, in the hallway, curled up beside a fan. The way Jimmy, before he was old enough to know what was happening to his body, let alone his sister's, had been taken in unto the fold.

It was dark, and I was asleep in our room. The swamp cooler was spinning, because it was hot, and you could feel the sky filtering through the drapes. At night, with everyone asleep, the house could have belonged to anybody.

Where were you?

In bed. I was in bed asleep; I was asleep in bed listening to the heat. In Arizona, August is the time for change—the season of monsoons. Daddy was coming down the hallway, and you could tell his step. It was heavy and damp, and Mom was asleep. Passed out, somewhere. I heard Jimmy's door open and knew I hadn't warned him.

Yes.

So I went into the hallway. I went out into the hallway and said, *Daddy. Daddy?* and he said, *Go to bed,* and I whispered, *No, Daddy, can we? You know, can we tonight?* and then he hit me, and then he hit me again, always on the body, places not supposed to show, and then he went in to bed.

But not to Jimmy's. In a way, he didn't do it that night to anybody. Not that night, but he did one night when I was afraid of paying any more attention. He slipped inside Jimmy's room and made us listen to the sound of it.

When May flew out to visit, on Easter, she brought us all presents from New York City. Her hair was yellow now and she'd had surgery on her face to make her cheeks look hollow. She said, after a while, nicely, that Jimmy and I couldn't come and live with her until we came of age.

The history of nations is determined by our natural resources—those raw materials by which one discovers energy, commerce, and universal greed. Irony, for example, makes for a poor return, and sarcasm is always cheap. What's of value, I now know, is that I grew up believing it was my fault. *Jimmy?* Yes, because I never did tell him. I mean I drove all the way across the California desert with Jimmy in a stolen car, and I never did tell him what Daddy did to me. I never did tell him that he wasn't sitting in that car all by himself.

Months pass, and Evangalene becomes more and more interested in the voice. The voice that is telling her this story.

No, I say.

"No, tell me about the voice. What does the voice look like?"

The voice belongs to a girl, of course. She is an eight-year-old girl wearing shorts beneath her skirt to keep the boys from seeing her underpants during gym and recess. The skirt is purple, like her sweater, the same sweater she will grow into and wear to cheer her up when she becomes cold in Yuma, Arizona. Suddenly, I am desperately afraid this may be the wrong answer.

"Purple," Evangalene says, smiling. Always she is smiling.

"Purple," I say.

"Where is she," she says.

What?

"Close your eyes. Close your eyes and take a minute. Tell me," she says, smiling, "precisely where she is."

And it is true, I think. I know precisely where she is. But to comfort an inner child, you must first believe in comfort. In sympathy, and none of us is ever special. We live each day longing to be more, don't we? *Don't we?* Sympathy is what tries to make us special, and if we believe in it, we believe we may be deserving of something other than our lot. Surviving, nothing more or less, which is to say, weeks pass into months, and later seasons. Winter has been cold and brutal, and meanwhile the future is unfolding in the center of my lap, here in my den, where I sit holding a glass full of vodka and ice, looking out the window. People are rehabbing the three-flat across the street; a couple years ago, it was a tremendously successful crack house. Now the prostitutes on the corner have turned out their summer clothes, and I am living here alone with my leather sofa. At night, looking out the window, I hold my glass in the center of my lap and tell myself I will not cry, and at work I have taken another leave of absence. My lover, who has since left me for New York City, and a few more figures to his salary, is spending an awful lot of time dining out with friends and his ex-wife.

Things, he says to me on the phone, over Christmas, are pretty swell. We're getting along real well together.

And then he says, "June? June, are you okay?"

This half, then the other; the good and also all the bad. Some things I don't want to find out, no matter just how long it has been, and still I know I'm going to. The truth is, I don't know what to believe in anymore. The Future or the Past. The here and now, as my lover used to say, requires Valium and Faith, but Daddy believed in months of the year, and in naming them: May, June.

June, honey. Fetch the paper. Kiss me quick, June. Bring me another can of beer, June.

Sometimes I wish he'd called me April, which always is the cruelest. I am sitting now on my leather sofa, looking out into the street, which is warm enough for spring, and knowing that I could have been someone other than I am. When Evangalene asks all over again what started this—what, she means, has brought my life to surface now, I know precisely what she's getting at, though of course she doesn't know the half of it. Yin, Yang; two peas in a pod. A woman and a man. So on.

Also, the answer always changes, especially in fairer weather. Most recently I have decided it is because Daddy's still alive, though slowly he is also dying. My daddy lies in a hospital bed in Phoenix, Arizona, *Good Samaritan,* with tubes stuck deep inside his throat. By now he must be yellow as a spoiled fish. His teeth sit neatly in a bedside drawer, along by the vomit pan and surgical gauze. And to tell the truth, instead of merely keeping it inside, it would not bother me to know that he was dying if he were still at least halfway lucid.

"He's out of his mind," I say to Evangalene.

Who smiles, meaning, Wasn't he always? I mean, that of course is the impression I have, June. Though clearly you know more than you are telling.

"No," I say. "He's out completely. He doesn't know who anybody is and he will not die. He will not die, Evangalene. He will not die!"

"Of course. We have to make room for him."

"No."

Of course, smiling. And suddenly I know that Evangalene *does* know the half of it, and the other, because in this life imagination can be more powerful than even incest.

It makes me feel foolish and weak for taking so long to discover this.

When the chips are down, who are you going to trust? Probably, you can imagine it makes me want to kill him.

Who?

Everybody, though mostly first myself, and sometimes when I call my lover I still ask him to forgive me. Now, sitting in Evangalene's office, that tidy well-lit space with the cozy plants . . . now and for the first time in years I do not consider suicide daily. Never, never have I admitted this to anybody.

"June," my daddy said, often. "June, you must always do just what we say."

More and more frequently May calls and asks me if I'd like to contribute. She means to the doctor bills; cancer grows increasingly expensive, though payment plans are currently still available. She means, Health care is a booming industry, and it is we, the sins of our father, who are going to have to foot the bill. Sometimes she asks me about psychotherapy; she has recently read somewhere that Winnie the Pooh is a case study in addiction.

"You know, all that honey?" She says, keeping me company, "You know AARP is the largest voting bloc in the country? It's one thing to screw the country up, but quite another to hang around on life support! With Alzheimer's!"

She has a point: modern medicine has made it difficult to

die; sometimes I worry we are all going to be here for a very long time. Even so, I'm thinking, how can anybody hate her family?

What I want to do is explain it all to May. I want to discover the source of my despair, and I want to explain it to her thus: just because our forefathers decided to have children with our mothers doesn't mean they should have. What seemed proper then horrifies me now. Like our daddy, tying on a bender, his semen sodden and full of booze; or our mom, decorating her house with brass and wicker. I learned to dance in the second grade, beneath the carport with my daddy's best friend, Neil. Neil had long shiny black hair and liked to call me *darling*. Later, after Daddy became upset, he slapped Neil upside the head and then, accidentally, knocked him out cold with his can of beer. I remember Daddy explaining that he was sorry, but even so only he was allowed to love me like that. We were all eating hamburgers in Yuma, Arizona, and he still had a mouthful. Neil was sitting by the pool, which wasn't yet quite empty. My daddy's best friend was sitting by the pool eating his hamburger and paying us no mind.

"No," I say to May, even more assertively, though we will always be separated by long distance. "I do not wish to contribute. I just want him to die and leave us all alone."

"It's a grieving process," May says, exclaiming. "Be glad it's going to be over soon! You can get on with your life!"

And then she says, hesitantly, because she's accustomed to awkward types of living, "How's Tim?"

She means the man who's dining out with his ex-wife in New York City, going to parties and making new friends and getting along just fine. She means, Aren't you seeing anybody new yet?

A woman and her therapist. If I fall in love with Evangalene, which I already have, will she someday be compelled to forgive me too? Her hands are soft and tender. Like me, she is not used to doing yard work. She wears thick furry sweaters and reminds me of a bear.

May no longer has her looks, though she's still tall and beautiful. She dates wealthy foreign men and never talks about her family. Occasionally, and once I came of age, we would take trips together to Mexico, and Spain, sometimes Madagascar. We would take trips alone and talk on the beach and she would tell me that Daddy wasn't such a bad man. He just couldn't hold a job. He didn't love his wife. He should have lived in Paris.

Once she told me she even missed him.

"Yes," I told her. "You certainly did."

"In a way," she said, almost wistfully. "You know, in a way I'm kind of sorry that it never happened to me."

"Yes," I said. "So am I."

As for Daddy, he doesn't know what he is missing, either; he still believes he is going to dance with me at my wedding. If his mind were still alive then possibly I could tell him? Daddy threw May out of the house for not coming home early enough Christmas Eve. She was sixteen and learning to sew and he was still employed. I was seven, maybe. Then she came home late, and he took away the presents she had brought. He took her by the wrist and began to scream, and eventually she took her presents back and broke away for New York City. Unlike most girls from Yuma, Arizona, who leave home for New York City, May didn't become a prostitute in Cleveland. Not even Syracuse. Instead she went to New York City and became a model and learned to put a pretty face upon her past.

My boyfriend, the one I had in Yuma, before I met the Christian, his name was Daniel. He said normally he liked pretty girls, better, but he was willing to hang around with me. Actually, he didn't know who or even what he liked. I didn't know it then, but I do know now some of his other half. That is, I know the things his parents did to him, too.

His father was in the Air Force and often flew aging fighter aircraft overhead.

"Okay," says Evangalene. "Why don't you tell me about the voice."

"You mean who I am?"

"I mean who is speaking. What I mean, June, is who is speaking to me now?"

You see I knew already I was pregnant. That night, that night we left Yuma with our daddy sitting at the table, waiting on us to bring him back his bottle, we drove fast. We drove fast with stolen license plates, and May was in New York City, posing in lacy underwear, beginning to make a name for herself. We drove toward Buckeye first because we didn't have a map, and then I found a sign that pointed us in the general direction of Los Angeles. My boyfriend had been to California once, Hollywood, where people made movies and millions and millions of dollars. I didn't think I'd make much money, but I knew it was also warm in California, that you didn't have to live inside the house in January, and I knew there was an ocean there. I'd seen pictures of it, mostly on the TV, which tried to make it seem convincing. On the way, we stopped at a rest stop. One guy wanted to give me a twenty-dollar bill; we were somewhere near the middle of the California desert, and Jimmy began to cry. He was sitting in the car, crying, because he hadn't eaten anything for days, which was the only time he ever made any noise, crying, and then the man said, "Come on, girl."

The man didn't have any tattoos along his arms. He smelled bad and needed a shave, but he was wearing a suit, too. "My daddy's a cop," I said. "Fuck off."

He laughed, as if he almost believed it. Jimmy honked the horn, and then I did some minor calculations. So far, we had only been gone half a day, and this was something I was fairly confident I could leave behind me at the border. I looked at Jimmy, sitting in the front seat, staring at the steering wheel. It didn't seem improbable, or even all that unusual, and then I said, "Mister, it would take a lot more than twenty."

The Christian boyfriend who liked my foster parents, he once told me he'd been saved since he was thirteen, and I said, "You're pretty lucky."

Evangalene says children of dysfunctional homes lack ritual, so now at the first of each month I always bring her a new plant in addition to my check: I'm thinking that after the first few times, it began to make sense. Sometimes I wore my purple sweater to school and sat on the lawns watching the sky. Each day, I have since realized, it is possible to see things differently. And then one day I couldn't find my sweater.

"Okay," says Evangalene, impatiently. "The voice."

I'd sit on the lawns and wait for Daniel to show up. Sometimes he'd ask me to do it in his car so he could say he liked it. Once, he cried in my arms, and I held him, tightly, because I knew that someday I was going to miss him. He'd look at the marks on my back, and legs, and ask me if it hurt; he did a lot of angel dust which made him unpredictable. You never knew exactly just what kind of pharmaceuticals you were buying back then. Drugs were still relatively expensive.

"Pharmaceuticals," I tell Evangalene, looking for the bright side. "And Gene Therapy. It's not too late for somebody still to make a killing."

As for the Christian boyfriend, he liked me to do things to him, too, and this was in a different state. Soon, only one thing left was sinful, and eventually I escaped and took a leave of absence and sent my lover back to his ex-wife. Then I spent twelve months watching CNN and learned, essentially, that it was time for change. I watched women march in Washington, DC, with signs that read *Get Bush Out Of Our Bush!* I watched downtown Chicago become evacuated three days before April fifteenth because of crumbling infrastructure; my accountant was instructed by the federal government to stamp *Chicago Flood* at the top of my return in order to escape penalties for being late. When a woman is late, it often means she's going to have a child. Do you really want to know the other half? After Pat Buchanan threatened to take our cities back, *M-16s at the ready,* even Bernie Shaw grew inarticulate and vague, and sometimes the phone would ring with news from people I still knew at work. Sometimes, I read badly written well-intentioned books about adult children of adult children, and when Ross Perot withdrew from the race, I knew even then he was going to come back in; sometimes, it feels good to make yourself feel bad, especially when you can still afford to. Nonetheless, I told myself, again and again, sometimes reading, sometimes weeping on my leather sofa, *it's time for change,* and Clinton went on MTV; the economy continued to flounder, obviously; the Olympics finally came along and provided some relief. In a few months a former POW running for vice president will forget to adjust the volume on his hearing aid.

Evangalene, I want to say, prepared now to make a joke. Where have I come to?

She is smiling, nodding, pretending to know precisely what I mean, though I can tell she's growing restless. Eventually she smiles and shakes her head, sadly, meaning I'm no longer doing the hard work I am supposed to. Like the American public, she wants to get back to the real issues.

And so I take a breath. I take in the city view from this high office and say, finally, "Except for being repeatedly violated as a child, I have never failed at anything."

Until now. Now we're finally getting somewhere. When the Chicago Bulls won the NBA, the people of the city rioted, just like Los Angeles, and it was possible to see most of the events in color from my living room. And maybe it *is* time we make a scene. Perhaps I know that I am getting better? After all, my daddy is going to die soon. I will never know what happened to my mother. Jimmy, though he is dead, no longer has to wonder why. Sometimes May sends me post-cards from Morocco and New Orleans. She has recently dis-covered a book, *Self-Pleasuring for Life,* and recommends it to me highly.

The voice, Evangalene is saying. *Tell me about the voice.*

But I don't know if I can believe in this.

Speak up, Evangalene says, gently. *Tell me what you mean.*

She means she knows I'm scared. I am scared because the voice belongs to that same little girl. She is a small girl, maybe eight, and wearing purple shoes. She is playing with her little brother, Jimmy, who doesn't like to speak. When I ask Jimmy why he never talks to me, Jimmy shrugs his shoulders and smiles.

"Are you mad at me?"

"No," he says, shrugging. "I'm Jimmy."

"I'm June," I say, holding out my hand. "Pleased to meet you."

We play some more in the yard, like a dream and very happily, before Daddy calls us in for supper. He is smiling, clean-shaven and content, and when we come running to the door he lifts us up into the air.

What does she want?

She wants to be lifted up into the air. She wants to feel better and she wants to tell Jimmy she is sorry. She is sorry, only Jimmy is far away, and she can't tell him she is sorry.

But where is she? Where is she right now?

She is lost. She is lost and she is found.

But June, why don't you just ask her to step outside? Here, among the living?

Finders keepers; the real issue has always been the way we live and die and teach ourselves to cross the street. Later, after I have moved away and begun to wean myself off the medication, I will listen to Al Gore give a speech. I will lis-ten to him explain to the beholden that Bill Clinton won this election because he was also willing to lose. Then, time moving on, then they will both lose: after Monica Lewinsky, one gate too many. And Al Gore, after calling for a recount, will spend a photographic op with his family in black turtle-necks playing football.

Touch, they say. *Let's play touch.*

It seems so very simple, really. The woods are dark and deep, and I will always be close enough to step inside: this is what I did, and where I am, and this is what I know. One day I made up my mind while walking home from school to make my life a better place; I was seventeen, and pregnant, and so I looked for an opportunity and ran with it. I ran with my silent younger brother and our daddy's station wagon. Then I ran with it elsewhere, to graduate school, to sound investments and comfortable furniture, and in so doing I became successful and made a lot of money. Which is to say, I spent my childhood thinking I'd feel better once I came into my twenties; and in my twenties, I said let's just wait until our thirties; and in my thirties, I realized that things were never going to change, and it was nearly enough to kill me.

"I mean, we are not going to change the world," I say to June.

"I know," she says, smiling. "It's okay."

She is holding my hand, wearing her purple shoes and yellow dress; her hair is done up in a pony tail, the way I used to like it, and we are walking down Michigan Avenue. You can feel the wind kicking up off the lake and June is looking up at all the tall magnificent buildings. Now she squeezes my hand, stopping to catch her breath, and says, "But it's so beautiful!"

We have made it into summer, our namesake. Evangalene, a woman I am in love with, distantly, tells me I've been merely winded. She says I will learn to forgive myself, and maybe she is right, though for the moment I am not quite certain. Mostly I want to show my little girl the sights; I want to bring her up safely and I want to teach her not to be afraid.

Today, after ice cream, which I have not had in years, we will go shopping at Field's, and now we are crossing the Michigan Avenue Bridge which has long since been repaired. We are crossing over to Dearborn, wandering through the traffic, smiling at the cab drivers. June squeezes my hand and says, "You know, I'm really hungry."

The campaign is still under way, nothing is ever certain, especially the disasters which will happen next, and across the avenue a crowd is gathering. For some reason we are the chosen and elect. There are television cameras and photographers and bleachers; officers are riding around on horses, and June reaches out to pet one. The officer smiles at me—a disheveled woman in her thirties, her jeans slightly faded, fresh from her analyst's office and staring blankly at a horse. Now the officer checks his watch and moves along while the crowd gathers up its momentum, because now it's finally time: lunch hour, on a fine city day in the tallest city in the world. Everywhere, people are happy, taking in the sun, shirtsleeves and bright loose dresses and comfortable shoes. I pick June up, lighter than air, and set her on my shoulders; and there, not too far away, stands a platform, and now when I make out a plum-colored dress, I am hoping that it just may be Hillary—the first lady of the future. She is speaking into a microphone, saving her husband's voice, her own booming off the buildings, larger than life. We can't understand a word she's saying, though most of us would like to believe in something. Meanwhile, June folds her hands on top of my head, and I step up on my toes, hopefully, in order to reach a better view. You see, I have begun to open up my eyes. And all around me I am looking for a reason, and maybe a new lover, and other ideas I'd like to get to know. I think it's time to make some introductions. Because all around me is this gathering crowd, and no matter how you have been raised, when we all finally do decide to cheer, for a moment it may be just enough to lift your heart.

To Comfort

Laurie says she found me naked, in the garage, screaming. I was lying naked beside the garden tools and camping gear, my hands over my head, screaming. She pulled out a dusty sleeping bag to cover up my body.

I don't remember much. I remember being out of Fiorinal and looking for something to kill the pain. I thought maybe there might be some aspirin on the workbench, beside the paint thinner and wood chisels. Instead the bottle was full of miscellaneous screws, a habit I've inherited from my father, who taught me, among other things, to save always what might prove useful. The screws were scattered now across the cement floor, and I remember Laurie calling the hospital, talking to somebody, explaining my family history. I remember vomiting in a bucket full of sawdust, and then another we used to wash our cars. Because we each loved our work, which meant we were also fairly good at it, we owned a vehicle and cellular phone apiece. Actually, I drove a truck, and Laurie put me inside her car; she ran inside the house to fetch a pair of jeans, a fresh shirt, while I shivered and wept inside her long, red car with a telephone.

The ride to the hospital was swift but nonetheless interminable. Once, Laurie ran a red light, reached for my hand, and said, "Soon, Sweetie. We'll be there soon." And I remember panicking, amid the pain, now unforgivable, because my health insurance payment was going to be a day late—a delay caused by recent developments involving a fresh policy for a new, improved and less expensive life. I remembered things that happened to my mother and instructed Laurie to pre-date the check, as if it really were possible to go back in time. When you feel as if nothing will ever stop, especially a violent and catastrophic pain inside your head, it is possible to lose your senses, and I remember thinking if she had not been there to care for me, to hold my hand and drive me to Emergency, then perhaps I would have had no need for comfort. Perhaps I would have been unable to give this up, to describe the way she made me feel, and I remember rolling down the window, gently, in order to permit escape.

First, an IV. The CAT scan, according to the ER intern, revealed no tumors or bleeds. My intern, Dr. Itzpala, wearing freshly laundered scrubs, seemed to be a pleasant woman. I suspect she was preoccupied with other matters: Would she ever get the day shift? Had she been consigned to spend the rest of her healthy life nearby a moderately violent inner city? The suburbs are a far more comfortable place to practice, a little bit each day, until you learn to get the basic matters of this life right. If you get married, you can get divorced, try again just down the block. I've built a number of houses for single and affluent parents. I've built living quarters for nannies and extended relatives not yet diagnosed with inoperable cancer or Alzheimer's. When an aide appeared to remove my IV, and then to give me a shot, Dr. Itzpala asked me how old I was.

"Thirty-one," I said. "And counting."

She said, beginning to flirt, unfathomably, "Trouble at work? The sun's not even up." I realized she was a pretty woman—skin, hair and eyes. A boy's dream. I imagined someday dating her, sharing a cappuccino across a wooden table, and realized it would be impossible. She was a doctor, paid to care for the sick, entirely compensated elsewhere.

I said, "Sure enough."

"Caffeine? Alcohol? You've been drinking? This is the third time in six months. You seem like a healthy man?"

"Stress," I said.

"Ahh. Stress." She lifted my wrist, then set it back down, deciding.

"I have to catch a plane," I said, sitting up. Then I realized I was naked beneath the gown. Laurie came into the room, brushing aside the curtain, asking how I was. She had been crying and, probably, talking on the telephone to her lover. She kissed me on the forehead, dead center, with the intent to cure.

My intern wrote out a prescription. The morphine hit suddenly, a wave designed to capsize, and I fell back onto the table. Dr. Itzpala turned to Laurie and said, pleasantly, I'd need more tests. She asked Laurie if she could sign some forms. I closed my eyes and slept, deeply, with my wife watching over me, holding my hand.

When I was nine my mother died of brain cancer. It sounds ridiculous, cancer of the brain, like what you might say as a kid about somebody stupid, so and so's retarded, or got *cancer of the brain,* but if you had seen my mother, lying on the couch, with cancer of the brain, you would have been filled with a legitimate and terrifying fear. You would have seen my mother, and the way she fingered her scarf, and you would have seen her eyes, which were blue, and her long slender fingers—the nails bitten to the quick. You would have seen her holding me to her side, whispering stories, one after another in order to distract us from the unutterable truth: she was dying a vicious and insidious death, and she was not yet even forty. And when I told my intern, Dr. Itzpala, that I was thirty-one years old, I realized I had become the same age as my mother the year I was conceived. It was the first time I understood that I was going to be required to spend the rest of my life as an adult, and I will tell you the

God's honest truth. It does not bother me that my mother died of cancer, as most people in this life will; what bothers me is that I watched it happen, the cancer eating away first her brain, and then her mind, while I stood by her side and fed her lukewarm soup. I watched my mother die and then I watched my father fall apart—a stone wall, absent any mortar, caught by the recurring tremors of a fault line. Now he, too, was dead, and Laurie and I were flying east to attend his funeral.

On the plane, I sat drugged and alert, as if embarking into a dream, and fully welcome to the possibilities: such is the virtue of a lingering narcotic. Laurie had packed quickly for us both while I took a shower. There was no cold water, of course. In Phoenix, you wait until November for a cool bath. Then I called my foreman with some last-minute details. We were laying a new foundation on Mummy Mountain, and the county surveyors still needed to confirm our specs. Three months from now, the house would be worth over two and a half mil, and somebody would be properly mortgaged to the throat, and then we'd have a small party—beer, hot dogs for the crew, flowers for the girlfriends and wives—in order to start in again. We had custom orders booked for the next two years. In general, I had made a mint, done myself proper, and spent the night inside the hospital again because I'd had another headache.

Laurie drank water, which wouldn't make her sleepy; she kept her hands folded on her stomach, just above the seatbelt. It had been nearly two years since I'd had any wine, or beer, which I specifically remembered now, being on a plane, and wanting a good deal of each. Strictly reflexive, that instinct. I quit drinking because I was afraid if I didn't then someday I would have to. As for my father, he had driven his boat onto the dock, which ruptured a gasoline tank. The gas had spilled out and been ignited by his cigarette. People saw the explosion across the bay. Nobody bothered to see if he'd been drunk, which of course he was. My

brother, Joel, was flying in from Atlanta, where he managed
a Latin American portfolio which had recently lost a third of
its NAV. Mexico, he said, appropriating the spin, was going
to remain volatile for at least another six weeks.

"Hey," he said. "These are dangerous times."

His accent had become increasingly Southern. He'd been
at school when Mom died. Choate, from which he'd gone to
Princeton, then on to the University of Chicago: he'd been
pedigreed and well-groomed for the purpose of taking excessive risks with other people's life savings. He had three kids,
one of whom he'd named after me. Two years ago, he'd
asked me to recommend an architect.

On the phone, he said, "You and Laurie still intending to
split the farm?"

"Still intending," I said.

"Should've had some kids, Little Brother. Collateral."

He was waiting for us at the gate in Newark. Laurie ran
ahead, wrapped her arms around his vast girth, equine in
scope, and kissed him on the cheek.

"Quite the little get-together," he said, nursing an airport
Scotch and water. "Little Brother, you look like hell."

"You get a car?"

"A big one. Two-seater. S'posed to have a loud radio,
even. A CD player!"

"I can't drive," I said.

"No," said Laurie, taking my hand. "Of course not."

My father often drove drunk and did not approve of music.
Over the years he had become a frightened, lonely, increasingly psychotic man. He lived alone on Barnegat Bay with
his cigarette boat and two Labradors. Mornings, he'd walk
along the Jersey shore, his dogs following along, playing in
the surf. That's pretty much all I knew about him anymore.
Once, he'd drawn a knife on me, Christmas vacation; at the
age of fifteen, apparently I'd said something inappropriate.
Occasionally, he'd call me in the middle of the night, ram-

bling. In the car, driving, Joel asked Laurie questions about immigration policy. Clearly he held his own opinions. He had some new theories, too, about our father—the loneliness, the shame, the genetic contributions of sheer lunacy. Meanwhile, I sat in the back, still riding the crest of my Fiorinal, measuring the traffic, which didn't seem all that much different from the traffic back in Phoenix: people had accidents most anywhere. Before Laurie fell in love with a man named Hector Lopez, she was angry with me for not wanting to have a child. She was ripe, she said. She was ready to burst.

We were sitting on the roof, watching the sky—our own private sundeck. It's the place where we first celebrated after I decided to go out on my own. Laurie, just home from work, had removed her blouse and bra. She had kicked off her shoes, her feet up on a crate. She put her hand on her belly, turned to me, and said, "Tell me you don't want to make love to me. Tell me, Mr. Hammer and Nail, you don't want to raise a little bambino."

It was a pretty sight, for a moment a tempting idea. There was a blanket nearby. My wife, among other things, is a handsome woman. She likes to camp. She likes to play softball. Mornings, she likes to roll in the proverbial hay. "Ohh," she'll say. "Make me late for work."

It's a good marriage, I've always thought so. I said, admiring the fine sky, "I don't want to be a dad. You know that."

She stood, suddenly angry. She kicked at my chair with her bare feet. "I'm serious, Neil. We're running out of time here. I'm running out of time."

"It flies, I know. People have kids when they're fifty."

"No," she said. "No, you don't know. I want to have a baby. This is not negotiable. This is not, *maybe someday.* This is serious. I want to have a baby while I'm still young enough to play with it."

"What? You gonna quit your job? You gonna start a day-

care? I'm not. You want a kid, go volunteer down in Guada-
lupe. Pick a dozen."

"Lots of couples figure this out."

"Yeah, and look at their kids. Good, decent kids all shot
up with crack and charge cards. Drooling in designer
strollers pushed by Guatemalan nannies. So nice, such good
people, those kids."

"You're not even willing to try?"

"No. I'm not."

"I don't need your permission, you know. I don't have
to—"

"Laurie, you do that—you get yourself pregnant on purpose—I'll divorce you."

I'd never spoken like that, and I meant it. It was the last
time we made love, that night, after we made up, gingerly.
Sex often made it easier for me to apologize, and while I was
willing to apologize for what I'd said, I wasn't about to
change what I believed. I spoiled it, too, that night. I kept
myself far away from her, even naked, in the center of our
bed, and after that argument, after her implicit threat, and
the fact of an earlier abortion with a college lover, I was
afraid she'd actually go and do it—allow herself to become
pregnant, slip a pill into the toilet, one day, then another. So
I began to go to bed after she fell asleep. I'd wake before the
first light, get a jump-start on the day. And she began coming
home late from her office, smelling all musky and damp, at
times oddly euphoric. Sometimes, she didn't come home at
all, and I'd go into the study, fall asleep there over blue-
prints. One night, she got drunk, and said, "Just because
your family is entirely screwed up doesn't mean ours has to
be." Then she threw her glass of wine at me.

"Look at you," she said. "You're afraid of a little wine. It's
wine," she screamed. "It's just white wine!"

A few days later, maybe even a week, I left the site early
and drove to her office. It was August, and hot—over a hun-

dred and twelve, the third day running. I'd thought, *Lunch,* but she wasn't in her office, which was halfway up the second-tallest building downtown. I took the elevator to the fern bar on the third floor and there she was, at a table with a tablecloth and nice crystal, sitting across from Hector Lopez. I recognized him from a couple parties for the city politicians. He was sensitive-looking and handsome: movie-style kind, in an expensive suit. The hostess frowned at me—jeans and boots, dusty—and I put my fingers to my lips.

"I'm spying on my wife," I said.

"Oh," she said, professionally. "Would you like to see a menu?"

"Not really."

"Really," she said. "I think you should at least have a menu."

My wife's back was to me. I could see her bra-strap beneath the fabric of her dress—one she had picked out for me to give her for her birthday. She was holding Hector's hand beneath the table. I watched him smile, say something, and begin to laugh. He had generous eyes and I knew then they were lovers. I returned the menu to my good hostess, left the restaurant and went to my truck, sat there, stewing in the heat, which was insufferable. It felt good, suffering like that. I imagined them at the Hyatt, later, making love. I imagined Laurie's throat, the vein which always begins to throb; her eyes, blinking like a blind woman's. I hoped Hector would be good to her—not just now, his mouth on her breast, but later, after the thrill of it all. Then I drove to my lawyer's office. I broke up a meeting, briefly, and told him to begin drawing up the papers.

"Jesus," he said, stepping outside of his office. "Not you, too?"

"I just need to get things rolling," I said.

"You okay? You need a drink?"

"Ed," I said. "You got business in there."

The hallway was full of plants and refrigerated air; I was beginning to chill and felt instantly stupid. I realized that, while we'd done an awful lot of business together, had spent weekends camping with our wives along the Mogollon Rim, this guy didn't know me any better than I did. He'd made out my wills, and I'd built on an addition to his ex-wife's house. He'd set up a trust fund for my brother's kids and had advised me, wisely, to stay away from variable life.

"Well I could use a drink," Ed said. "That's for damn sure."

"Mr. Hollander," said his secretary, a woman old enough to date my father. "Mr. Hollander, you just need a good night's rest. You're upset, that's all."

"Laurie," Ed said. "Laurie—she know about this yet?"

"Of course she does, Ed. How can anybody not? You think people get divorced by accident? You think people just wake up and they're God damned separated? You think people just don't know any better?"

"You're upset," Ed said. "You're—"

"Call me at work," I said. "From now on."

"Okay."

"Laurie," I said. "She'll be needing a good lawyer too. Maybe you could recommend one. If it's not a conflict, that is."

"Ahh," Ed said. "Conflict."

We live in a no-fault state. The legal phrase Ed Alexander would use to describe our divorce is *irreparably broken,* but a marriage is not a car, or for that matter a board; an idea cannot simply break like that: it has to be first worn out by years of self-reliance and neglect. And it's not that I didn't want to spend the rest of my life with Laurie—I did, unequivocally. But I also didn't want to deny her the possibility of having a family proper. At the time, I also wanted to hurt her badly. And Hector Lopez, I eventually realized, was a decent man; otherwise she never would have been with him. It wasn't about me as much as I might have hoped, which of course made me feel even worse. Your wife starts sleeping with the local politicos and, what, you're going to start taking out the garbage? You're going to pick up your sweaty socks and buy a necktie?

That night I checked into a hotel. I walked down a filthy block, stepped into a liquor store and bought a fifth of bourbon. I felt criminal, doing that; I felt the need for explanation, and I tried to make a joke, but the man I was speaking to couldn't hear me for all the bulletproof glass. He slipped my change beneath the glass and turned to face a television. The bottle felt heavier than I remembered. I went outside onto the street, whiskey in hand; there were Chicanos sitting on the curb, smoking a joint, another passing a quart of beer. I went back to my hotel, stripped out of my clothes, took a hot shower, and sat on the bed, watching the news with the sound turned off. There were riots replaying in LA, and a man was having his face beat with a brick. After a while I held the whiskey in my hands. I pictured myself drunk and ridiculous. Mostly, I wanted the sweet comfort of oblivion, which is what most everybody wants, so long as he doesn't have to pay for it. It's one thing to love your wife, and quite another to realize she may be better off without you. Love makes even the pure of heart—or hard—complicitous. And so while I took my good and hot pathetic bath, I did not open up that bottle. Instead I drank half a dozen glasses of water. I took another scalding shower. Then I put the whiskey in a drawer, beside the Gideon bible, and put on my clothes. I laced up my dusty boots and drove home.

I drove home from the motel, fast, still needing to feel as if I had direction. Laurie stood in the kitchen, putting pasta in the oven, probably just to keep warm for me. Usually I called if I was late.

"Hi," she said, kissing me. "Where you been, Mister?"

I said, "Want to take a ride?"

We went to the truck and I drove off, toward Camelback,

up the mountain. It was dark by now. Laurie sat with her feet propped on the dash, dusty as the road. The wind blew in her long hair. The neighborhood, expensive and assiduously quiet, rose into the hills. I pulled up beside a backhoe and stepped out. In the starlight, you could see our office trailer—*Hollander Specialty Homes*—and Laurie came around the truck. She was in her sandals, and I told her to watch for nails.

"In the dark," she said. "Uh huh."

I took her by the hand and led her to what would someday be a front door.

She said, pretending to knock, "Why don't you make one of these for us?"

"Taxes."

"Housecleaning," she said, laughing. She turned and took a breath. "You're mad at me about that drinking thing. That thing I said that night?"

"No."

"You should be. It was awful. I was awful."

"It was true."

We walked through the living room, the den, out toward the pool, which had been dug into the mountain. The house, complete, would comprise over five thousand square feet. I reached down for a level and kneeled to check a sill.

"Here," I said. "Look."

"What?"

I showed her. You could just make out the fluid bubble, resting dead center. The house was going to be okay. "I was afraid," I said. "I wanted to check it."

"It's level?"

"It's level. When it's off, when the sill isn't level, the house goes up crooked. The joints don't agree. Nothing trues."

"A house divided cannot stand," Laurie said.

"No," I said. "That's a myth. Fact is, most stay up for generations."

She began to cry now. She took my hand, let it go. She stood in front of the pool. There was scrap inside it now—two-by-fours and skids and electrical conduit. We'd thought about actually putting one in our own yard. It's not as if we couldn't afford it.

"It's my fault," she said. "It's all my fault."

"No," I said. "It's nobody's."

She began to cry harder, punching me. "It's got to be somebody's!"

"My dad," I said. "He used to blame me. Said it was my fault for being born. Then he began to blame himself. He made sure we'd hate him. He bought a liquor cabinet and sent me off to prep school."

"Jesus," she said. "So your dad was crazy. So what? So you won't make love to me?"

"Do you want me to?"

"No," she said, blinking. "I don't think so."

"I spoke to Alexander. He's drawing up the papers. He said he'd recommend a lawyer. No fault."

She laughed now. She wiped her eyes and laughed really hard. "You," she said, pointing. "You're a pillar, you know that? You're hard as fucking brick."

A migraine gives off warnings: for me, a patch of light, usually in the left eye, which then begins to cloud your vision. It's caused by a constriction of the blood vessels in the brain, and over the years I'd discovered ways to take care of myself and to spot them coming: usually a couple Midol—aspirin, and 500 mgs of caffeine—and then a hot cup of coffee in a dark, silent room. Fiorinal, deliciously habit-forming, worked well; morphine simply sent you to the moon. Apparently, I'd inherited the affliction from my mother, whose brain cancer was in fact first diagnosed as another migraine. It was like learning to live with a bomb, always ticking, and a constant reminder to be grateful when you couldn't hear it. It was important, Laurie said, that I learned to control my blood pressure.

The morning of my father's funeral in Point Pleasant, New Jersey, Laurie and I woke early. The beach was silent and asleep. My father's dogs rooted around in the sand, digging for clams. In the clear vision of the aftermath, and having spent the night together with us, instead of at the kennel, the dogs no longer seemed disoriented or betrayed. Laurie and I were going to take them both, in order to save them from being put down or, worse, split up. Joel already had a dog his kids refused to play with. I pictured myself at a job, tape in hand, my dogs patrolling the lot: the independent contractor. The water, Laurie said, dipping her foot into the sea, was cold. She unbuttoned her blouse and called, "Come skinny-dipping. Come skinny-dipping with your wife."

"This is New Jersey," I said. "It's illegal."

"No," she said. "It's your last chance."

The water was cold—brisk, like a spring shower—and full of salt. Growing up near the beach, you appreciate the simple things: a clear sky and a fire, a pretty girl to swim with. We swam out first a hundred yards, then another. I'd forgotten what it was like, being in the water. The sun was rising dead ahead, and there was the sky, and the water, and I realized I had at least for the moment become a happy man.

"You're smiling," Laurie said, over the waves. "About time, Mister."

"It's too late," I said, wishing it no longer was. I thought of my wife swimming in a chlorinated pool with a man named Hector Lopez. Eventually, he would run for office—district attorney, which would naturally lead to other offices.

"Oh God, Neil," Laurie said, sputtering. "It's always too late."

"You're having an affair," I said. "I didn't start that."

"I'm divorcing the only man I've ever loved," she said. "You tell me. You tell me what's fair!"

Living together for eight years, we'd learned not only to think alike; we spoke alike, as well—a lexicon set in code, refined by years of common history. For example, we each believed in quick disclosure so long as nobody nearby was there to listen in: a man would turn to sex because it didn't require that he believe in anything; a woman, because to offer up the body was a less expensive item than her heart. It was something which would of course make perfect sense, so long as it were happening to another; after we were first married, I'd had my own summer of marital indiscretion. As for Hector Lopez, he was a good and decent man, but he wasn't going to steal away my wife unless I let him, and eventually we headed back to shore. The water had made us inexpressibly sad. Joel was standing there, a beer in his hand, his feet deep in the sand. Our clothes were piled up beside him. He was talking on the phone.

We scrambled, pushed by the waves. Laurie called to him, said *Turn around!* but he just smiled and waved. Now he pressed some buttons, shut the phone up, turned his back to us while pointing with his foot to Laurie's bra.

"Recognized this," he said. "Figured it was somebody's I knew."

"It's good," I said. "You should take a dip."

"Too much exercise," he said, peeking, not at me. "Just lost another two and a half mil. I'm telling you, Little Brother, stay out of places where people carry rifles. No revolutionaries. Good, basic rule."

Laurie reached for her blouse, began to button up; we shook sand from our clothes while Joel discussed the forthcoming collapse of bonds.

"Okay," Laurie said. "I'm decent."

"Of course you are," Joel said, turning. "You're rich. You're beautiful. Your husband should have been a fucking priest."

"Careful," I said. "Be very careful."

A thin woman, elderly, approached in her floral swimsuit. We didn't recognize her, as if we should have, but she claimed to know us. The sun had turned her skin to rawhide. She petted one of the dogs as if he might bite her, or were dead. Her hair may have been gray, she explained, but she played tennis often. She commented to us on the quality of the beach.

"Private, you know."

"Yes Ma'am," Joel said, folksy as pie. "Proud of it."

"I saw you, swimming like that. Good time, the morning. Just us early birds around. You're the Hollander boys, aren't you?"

Joel insisted that we were, and it struck me that she didn't know our father was dead. She had a bracelet around her ankle, the electronic type used for cattle and parolees.

"You know, Dear," she said to Laurie. "You know, everybody around here owns a telescope." She looked at me now, smiled, and said, "And your mother, too. Such good, nice people."

Which of course is what we Hollanders had become—good and nice, properly raised, exquisitely educated. My brother had an ulcer and stole sips of Pepto Bismol whenever he thought nobody was looking. I suffered from recurring migraines and was about to divorce a woman who had devoted her life's work to protecting the legal rights of aliens. Dressing for the funeral, which we'd arranged to last less than twelve and a half minutes, I remembered my insurance policy—a sudden wave of panic.

"Check's in the mail," Laurie said. "Why? Are you getting another headache?"

"No," I said. "I don't think so." I thought about my policy and preexisting conditions, the need for eternal vigilance. A reliable postmaster, the ability to send things through the mail—my policy would take effect any day, and for a while, at least until the separation took effect, our emerging fortune would be safe. As it was, that emergency room visit was going to set us—no, *me*—back at least a couple thousand.

"I'm glad he's dead," Laurie said, nodding into the mirror. "He was an evil man."

"You don't make money by spending it," I said, wanting to be angry. "That's what he always said."

"He did terrible things to you," she said. "He got beat up a little bit and decided to do his best to destroy you."

"He was my father. And you didn't have to come along."

"Of course I didn't," she said, straightening my tie. "And he didn't have to leave his estate to the John Birch Society. He didn't have to slap you from the grave. He didn't have to show up at our wedding with a gun!"

I'd forgotten about that, actually. Now after spending years threatening to kill himself, he'd finally gone and done it unintentionally. It was laughable, really. My father died alone because his children were no longer willing to come visit him, let alone talk to him on the telephone, despite their love for him. In the living room, waiting for us to finish dressing, Joel sat in my father's chair, beside my father's telescope, smoking. Joel said, looking up at me, in tears, "I am not going to feel guilty. I am not going to let him ruin my vacation."

Now he lifted his beer, as if in a toast, and said, "To propriety, Little Brother. To sweet and everlasting ruin."

Mercifully it was just us—my brother, my wife—at the burial site. A backhoe, parked in the distance, had dug the trench square. Joel had picked out a nice coffin which was guaranteed by a salesman in Linden, New Jersey, to last in perpetuity. Mostly, I think my father believed the rights of family entitled one to the privileges of abuse: it was the supreme gift of genetics complicated by tradition. Blood gave one the right to draw it from another at will, regardless of consequence; if you were family, my father reasoned, then you had to forgive, but after a while we simply didn't have anything left to forgive him with, and as a result my father died a lonely, bitter man, and then he left his sons behind to carry on his legacy. The choice, of course, was ours to make alone—like who you intend to love, in spite of the blood which has already been spilt, or what you choose to forget because of it—the blood, which we filter with our lives, slowly, one hopeful and irrefutable day at a time. And it struck me, then, staring at the lid upon my father's coffin, that we can be held accountable in this life only for what we know. And so knowing, then we simply have no other way to turn: we're going to have to try to live a decent life, which is to say: after my father was lowered into the grave, I stood behind Laurie and laced my fingers tight around her belly. It was firm, smooth beneath the silk. I nuzzled her neck and knew then, right then, that I wanted to take her back to the sea. That night, we would sit around the fireplace in my father's empty house, as if waiting for him to become a proper ghost. Joel would tell stories about him, sloppily, until Joel finally drank himself to sleep. Then, if Laurie would permit me, I'd begin to apologize: it would be the kind of reconciliation which might last for hours. In the morning, as the day grew ripe, we'd return to the beach; we'd bring the dogs, go swimming into the sea. My wife, I'd say, she likes the sea, and I'd swim a bit further out, waiting for her to come find me, which, thank God, she would. And we'd stay there like that, treading water, the space between us fluid and lit eternally by the sky. Because this was finally a place that belonged to both of us, and something even I was allowed to have: a second chance. And I knew then this was going to be my home. Because this was my wife, to have and to hold, just like that, and right before the mercy of the grave.

Light Rock

The graveyard is always quiet. Nights, when they call up for requests, you know that they are lonely. Sometimes, they are lonely and sad. Girls, worried about what they did wrong at prom. A married man, working as a security guard, looking out the window. At night, they always call Angelica, and always she is polite.

"Hi," she says. "This is Angelica."

"Will you play a song? For Joe?"

Her actual name is not Angelica, but Wendy. Her program manager once explained that it is often safer to be someone else. She once had a great-aunt Angelica who kept a secret diary, and this caller, a young girl, has been a regular for months—always calling in the middle of the night. Wendy imagines the girl small and quiet, living sleepily in a suburb with her radio.

"Of course I'll play a song for Joe. I'll play a song for you, too."

"That's okay. Just for Joe. I hope he's listening."

At first it was the music, and then later the idea, which drew her in, here to radio, and the songs she likes to play— nothing that fits too easily into a genre. Tonight a young sleepy girl wants to hear a song by Stevie Wonder, a song which still requires cueing up, not yet acquired by her employer on CD. Sometimes, listening to Mozart, or Haydn, Wendy begins to feel oppressed by mass marketing and publicity; music seemed far more driven, and less absolute, when one could listen to it privately with a king. It's an argument she has often with the rock star, Leon, who has briefly returned to Phoenix with his young wife, Sissy.

A long time ago, before Wendy became Angelica, she and Sissy went to school together; they shared a dormitory room and dreamed of writing novels. Now Sissy lives off her trust fund and lies often to her parents: most recently, she is writing a biography of her husband, though of course the book will not be written, let alone published, unless Leon becomes a born-again Christian or dies of AIDS. As for the here and now, Sissy wants to live happily with her husband, who is struggling, not altogether successfully, to remain faithful and kick his coke habit.

This morning, sitting around the kitchen table, drinking margaritas, Leon says, proudly, "There is nothing new under the sun."

"Cliché," says Sissy, nodding.

"Ecclesiastes," Wendy says. "All is vanity."

"Even clichés have become predictable," Sissy says. Now she giggles like a girl. In general she is a pale and tiny woman—a mouth the size of a small flower, or coin.

And Wendy, who has just returned home from her shift, sits awkwardly at the counter, watching her friends enjoy their breakfast. She is slightly hungry, though mostly she wants to finish off another glass of water with another Valium and then go in to bed. Lately she has been sleeping in the guest room, which Leon has also set up as a working studio. His guitars and keyboard lean against the wall, covered with dust. Wendy says, lifting her head, undoing the top button on her blouse, "How's the water?"

"Wet," says Leon, looking out at the pool. The pool is sitting there beneath the hot and rising sun. Inside the water is blue and clean, delicious. The water is just the way people like it, and now Leon says, raising his glass, "I suggest we spend the day celebrating the fine fact of water."

Sissy says, "Water, water everywhere. But don't forget the sunscreen!"

Wendy is standing now, holding her glass of water, beginning to sway. "I'm tired," she says. "God, I'm really tired. Did Paul call?"

Paul is Wendy's husband, who lives in New York City, working as an assistant tech director for a remarkably far off-Broadway play. He has lately decided he is not returning west, though Paul is also not certain he wants to stay with theater: mainly, it's hard to make a living. First DC, then Chicago, now this. Usually he calls late at night, while Wendy is in the studio, doing her own show. Based on the size of his phone bill, she is pretty certain Paul is sleeping with the girl he lives with. If Wendy moves to New York City next fall, as previously arranged, the girl is supposed to be moving out.

Sissy says, looking at the pool, "If you go, I'll follow."

Sissy means the water in the pool, which in this neighborhood is not uncommon. It takes Wendy a moment to realize what is meant—the pool, and all the clean water—and Leon is stroking his goatee, admiringly. Before she married Paul, in a small chapel near New Haven, somebody had told her it was time to take the plunge.

"Go," Leon says to Sissy. "Go."

"It's funny," Wendy says, blinking. "I'm not used to all this light."

In 1893, her great-aunt Angelica took a lover, in Memphis, Tennessee, who worked at the town bank. The banker eventually left his wife and caused a scandal; months later, a boy found the banker's body swinging in a barn. Today, the bereaved might sell the story to a television network, in the spirit of redemption, or revenge, but in 1893, her aunt, writing in her diary, asked merely for forgiveness. *It has been wrong,* Angelica wrote. *And I pray God forgives this wretched place.*

Mostly, a hundred years later, Wendy wants to feel clean and alive, lighter than air. In the water, she leans against the rim of the pool, her arms spread out onto the hot deck behind her. Her ribs feel sharp and alert. Years ago, swimming naked with her friends would have seemed impossible; she lets her legs float and reminds herself, repeatedly, that medication is often comforting. Leon, who is standing on the diving board, taking pictures, is not allowed to drink.

Sissy scoops a glassful of ice and throws it on the water.

"I love the way it floats," Sissy says. "Ice, I mean."

Leon says, "Where's the ice?"

"The house," Sissy says, pointing.

The house belongs to Sissy's family, though Wendy has been living here for the past three years. Sissy and Leon prefer to stay in LA, New Orleans and Manhattan, in that order. Sometimes, flying across the country, Leon will stop in Phoenix to spend a couple days. At first he brought women with him—girls, actually, future voices of the industry; he'd leave condoms on the couch, by the poolside. He has been in and out of detox twice in the past year alone. Sissy, of course, knows only about the detox, and it makes Wendy nervous, knowing so much about a man her friend has wed for life. On his latest video, you can see Sissy in the sidelights of Trump Plaza, swooning in adoration. If Leon's band goes on tour next fall, something which Leon does not want to do, then Sissy says she will go along to keep him clean.

"Assuming," Sissy said, laughing, "he's clean to begin with."

Leon always looks clean. He is returning from the house with a bucket of ice and a sophisticated camera. Usually, he keeps himself well-groomed and politely distant. Even when he's undressed, Leon looks more like a disinterested professor of art, or a successful architect, than he does a rock star. In Chicago, where he grew up, the Ukrainian Village, he spent a lot of time learning other trades—auto mechanics, drug dealing. The usual, he calls it, and since that time he has bought his mother several mink coats and a new pink house across the street from where he grew up. Sometimes, when Leon stops by on his way to Los Angeles, he visits Wendy's room at night. Usually he is wasted to his knees.

In the pool, admiring the water and the heat, Wendy says, "I have to sleep."

Leon says, adjusting a lens, "Paul wants a divorce. He made jokes about it last night."

"Paul always jokes about divorce," Sissy says. "He believes in monogamy."

"Like you?" Leon says to Sissy. He is looking at his camera, which seems to have a lot of switches and knobs. "Hold that, there."

When Paul says he wants a divorce, it means he's afraid that Wendy's going to leave him. Leon takes the picture, while Sissy holds, and smiles. Sissy is standing on the top step, also naked, looking like a little girl. She has no breasts to speak of, and she likes to shave. Charming, Wendy thinks. And sexually illicit. This tiny girl in her tiny body all grown up. She can't weigh more than ninety-three.

"Monogamy," says Sissy, "works only if you believe in it. And if you believe in it, then you simply cannot screw around without feeling guilty. And if you feel guilty, Leon, then you might as well get divorced, because who wants to feel what anybody else can have?"

"Like your husband," Leon says, nodding.

Sissy sits on the top step and splashes her face. She sets her elbows on her knees, her chin in her hands, and says, leaning forward, "It's not about sex, Leon. It's about *me*."

Wendy knows that Sissy has been loyal. Not once, Sissy claims, not once since her marriage to Leon has she been tempted by another. At the ceremony, in Buenos Aires, Madonna's secretary wore pink and blue. One night, after Leon hit Sissy in a Manhattan club, Sissy called Wendy at the studio. Sissy was sitting in her bathtub, fully clothed in club gear, using the cordless phone. There were bubbles everywhere, she explained, and it was then that Sissy said, "Sometimes, sometimes he's so right!"

Apparently, Leon had also hit a nerve. Once you married a man you were in love with, you weren't allowed to wish you hadn't. Otherwise, this was failure.

"I'll tell you a secret," Sissy had said. "Want to know a secret?"

"No," she said to Sissy. "Not really. Are you all right?"

"It's a big one, Wendy. It's a really big one."

"Maybe you should stay somewhere else. For tonight."

"His new record. It's a flop. A bomb. You know, like they say on Broadway? It won't even pay for the videos, and now they have to make another and use the Statue of Liberty. Then they say they have to go on tour, and Leon says, No. No, Sissy has to clean the house."

"Can you come visit? Come stay in Phoenix?"

"No," Sissy said, whispering, beginning to cry. "I *can't* come. That's the secret, Wendy. Don't you see? *I can't come.*"

Sometimes you have to let yourself let go. According to those who live there, the act of radio was invented in Murray, Kentucky, a place her great-aunt passed through on her way to Indiana. The family had been shooed away from Memphis by scandal and a legal writ. They settled once again in Bloomington, this time for a hundred years.

She thinks if a man thinks about divorce, then probably his wife does too. It starts with more than just a phone call. Paul, her husband in New York City, says it's safe and doesn't do anybody any harm. He often asks her to send money for the phone bill. Not *their* phone bill, but the bills he runs up on the 900 numbers. Hundreds of dollars a month. And while he never says the money goes to the phone company, she sends it nonetheless; if he is on the phone, she reasons, he is often harmless. Sometimes he special orders calls for her very own. A man will call her up at work, while she's in the studio, and ask her if she likes to sweat.

"I live in Phoenix," she might say. "It's not uncommon."

Once, a woman called, who pretended to take a survey. The woman called early on a Saturday while Wendy was still in bed; the woman said she was working on her dissertation and needed some random sampling. "Do you talk with other women often?" the woman asked.

She sounded pleasant, like a friend. There wasn't any static, and Wendy lay in bed, talking about herself and, after a while, lovers she had known.

"Do you like lingerie?" the woman asked, gently. "Would you describe the lingerie you're wearing now?"

None? You're wearing none?

That is when she knew it was a message straight from Paul. The woman was smooth and knew how to make you feel inspired, and hot, and far away from home. Even when he's drunk, Paul is always harmless on the phone. Sometimes he is even charming, and afterwards, the woman said she knew him very well.

"Though of course we've never met," the woman said. "I'm sorry, Wendy. But I can't give you my real name."

She knew exactly what she meant. Usually Paul won't remember what he's talked about unless it causes an awful lot of pain.

"I could leave him," Wendy said to Sissy. "We don't have to stay married."

They were sitting on the pool deck. Leon was on a flight to Denver, supposedly to do a final shoot for the band's forthcoming release of "Wicked Heart, Wicked Heart." It was a song Leon wrote to show Sissy he was sorry for hitting her in a Manhattan club.

Sissy took a sip of her iced tea, listening, because she was a friend.

"It's just hard because we're so far away," Wendy said, entirely by heart.

"You should leave him," Sissy said. "Sayonara, Baby."

If Sissy left Leon, she couldn't be in any more of his

videos. Leon has sung a lot of songs about his wife. He says it comes with practice.

"If I leave him," Wendy said. "I mean, if I decide to divorce Paul . . . if I do that, then what?"

"If you're someplace you don't want to be, you shouldn't be there. We could go to Graceland. We could meet Leon in Rome."

"I can't speak Italian," Wendy said. "Besides, he loves me."

"Of course he loves you. That's why it has to be your fault. You have to tell him what he already knows, Wendy. You have to do the hard part." Now Sissy looked across the yard, where there stood a gardener, landscaping. The gardener was trimming bougainvillea along the stuccoed cinderblock wall. Most likely, he didn't speak a word of English. Sissy said, "I know Leon doesn't love me. But at least he's faithful."

"Of course he loves you. He adores you."

"Yes, he does that," she said, reaching for her tea. "He adores me. He used to be pretty good at that, too."

"I believe in marriage," Wendy said. "I just don't believe it's possible."

"Of course it's possible," Sissy said. "Why else would it always go wrong?"

"You have to believe," Wendy said, nodding.

Sissy pointed to the gardener, admiringly. "Of course," Sissy said, pointing, "you also have to know when it's time to walk away."

Wendy has talked to men and women often, mostly at night, while playing songs for all the world to hear. *The Song of Solomon, The Book of Psalms*—the human voice was built to keep us out of danger. Desire, and the way it draws the body inward. Alone, living, one learns not to be excessive. To save and wait for rainy days. As a teenager, when she first realized she might be fat, and always lonely, she grew to trust her instincts. By the age of seventeen she was vomiting twice a day.

In Phoenix it rains only when necessary, and often not at all. After a while, desire becomes a matter of faith, which is nothing more than the hope of things yet unseen, like voices on the telephone. If Sissy is doing something wrong with Leon, then maybe she should read some books, maybe take a couple courses in communication. This evening, while Wendy was in the shower, Leon stepped inside the bathroom and asked her what she'd like for dinner.

Wendy reached to turn down the spray. The shower was enormous, large enough to swim in. Half of it turned into a Jacuzzi, and Wendy said, "Where's Sissy?"

"Taking a nap."

"I thought you were in Denver?"

"Took the Cessna," Leon says. "We have it for another month."

She reached for the shampoo. She thought of Paul, talking on the telephone. Most likely, Leon had flown to Denver just to meet his dealer.

"It snowed," Leon said. "Ruined the entire shoot." He looked at the floor, and then the towels.

"Wendy?" Leon said, looking up.

"Yes?"

"She's too good for me. Sissy. She's too good and she still can't live without me."

She poured too much shampoo into her palm and said, cautiously, "Maybe you should give her a try?"

And then he shrugged, turned into the mirror, watching her, and left.

It was the type of moment she will recall years later—a moment fraught with tenderness and lust—and tonight, on her way down the mountain, past the sturdy security office, and the sturdy man inside, reading, she listens to the radio.

There is music in the air, and pollen, and now there is a moment of silence, between songs—dead air.

Somebody at work clearly is not paying much attention. Her program director, a man who looks as if he is a deacon, has twice admonished her for deviating from the schedule. He threatens often to take her off the air. If it weren't for advertising, the world would be another place—far away, and maybe less expensive. It used to be she couldn't stand to be naked in front of anyone. Then she went to counseling, and spent a lot of time with Sissy. Among friends, we are taught, you are not supposed to hide.

When she and Sissy shared a dormitory room at a small, expensive college, they also shared their dreams: a lot of falling and running fast downhill. Together, Wendy and Sissy would grow up and become artists and have boyfriends who liked to break the smaller laws: boys who wouldn't shave closely and always smelled of tobacco and wine. They could all be Bohemians, and beautiful, and die from a life of poverty, later to be described by a fine new school of art. But after graduation, Sissy flew to Monaco, and Wendy went home to Bloomington, Indiana. Her father had died. The estate was in arrears. Men in ugly clothes repossessed the family station wagon, and then the farm equipment; the department stores were last to be sold off. Throughout the process, Wendy spent a lot of time doing volunteer work for the church.

She had read Boethius, had understood the whims of Fortune, which had now become a magazine. America, she soon discovered, did not pay much attention to the history of the world. One day, you're stealing car stereos on Lake Street, the next you're making popular entertainment and coming across a pair of Delco speakers. Even Leon has had a song or two on the charts. Ten years from now, someone might play one of the deeper cuts. *May 20th, 1993. Where were you?* . . . and tonight she is in the valley, which is dark and illustrated by light, the low-wattage ambiance of smog. If she stays in Phoenix, then she will not have a reason to leave it for her husband. Clearly, resurrection is the theme here. A second chance. Hollywood after Rehab . . . *Can't we try again?* . . . and she is driving through the city, down Twenty-fourth Street, with the top down. The air can carry radio and disease, water and even light. Living her life with Paul, however separately and alone, living this life has taught her to watch for the way light falls. The way it can instruct the stage to bend. Theater is light, Paul says. Life is dark.

On the air, she opens with that comment. It's late, she says, does anybody mind if she smokes?

Sound, she has always imagined, moves far more gently than illumination.

Eventually she spent a couple years in seminary, just to try things out; her advisor was coming out and very Theologically Correct. *God for the Environment. Christ for Disenfranchised Congregations.* When asked by her advisor if she had a calling, Wendy had said, "Sometimes I hear voices in my head. But I don't think that's exactly what you have in mind."

"You no longer wish to be ordained?"

"I believe in God," she said. "What's left to be ordained?"

She finished her degree, conspicuously taking the non-ordination route, and knew she'd never find a job. Nonetheless, people noticed she had gained some weight. A few days later, she stumbled into Paul, who was drunk—a social gathering for distant members of the college. He was doing summer theater, and bartending; in college they had slept together often. Her father had been alcoholic, the harmless type who drinks alone in order best to avoid his creditors, as well as his wife, who also drank, and Wendy had decided when she fell in love with Paul for the second time to never drink again, which made it hard, sometimes, living with

Paul: practice, and a lot of painful and late-night conversations. Eventually, a second summer theater ended right on time, and in the fall, they moved to Phoenix, because there she had a job selling time for a television network; they moved to Phoenix because he was going through a bad time, and because in Phoenix it was easier for him to go through a bad time all by himself. At least here he didn't know anybody. He wasn't going to lose any friends over it. The bad time lasted for several months. Each morning, Wendy went off to work.

"So I'm not doing Broadway," he would say, often, sitting in a comfortable chair. "At least I'm not teaching high school."

Sissy asked them to live inside of her enormous house, on top of Camelback Mountain, and sometimes Wendy knew Paul wouldn't mind teaching high school. Anything to get him up and off the mountain. Eventually, he began to work out; he bought some new clothes on the Visa and then one day decided he should try again. He was going to turn thirty soon. One last try before he gave it up for good and started building furniture. With all his experience on the set, most likely he could teach himself to build a coffee table, or a chair. It's not as if they were about to have kids. Wendy didn't want kids, but still she liked them. She still liked people who weren't afraid to blink. If she had been a better person, less self-involved, then maybe she could have some? At twenty-nine, she's had several root canals already. Her teeth are swollen with decay. She once went two years without a period. What they don't tell you in school about bulimia is this: it often feels good.

And now, in the morning, after finishing her log, she knows precisely what she wants to do, though she knows she will not do it. Even so, she wants to do it all over again—empty herself out, make herself clean. At first, as a young girl, you become friendly with your fingers—it only takes two—and then you learn to control the other muscles in your body. You teach your stomach to pay attention to your mind. You take it all in, and then you give it all back before anything can hurt you. Like a man who still wants to be your husband, living in a foreign city, already plotting another life for you. Like your best friend, decorating house in Manhattan or New Orleans. Like all those people who call up each and every night with their requests.

This one's going out to a good friend in Paradise Valley, you might say, because if they call you up, if they listen to you in the middle of the night, then they are always, always going to be good friends. Good friends, who have nothing left to hide.

In bed and still not quite awake, she knows that somebody else is in the room. She considers sitting up and feels a hand come across her mouth. The hand lifts, gently, and Wendy knows she doesn't have to be alert. The light is bright enough to sleep through. She could pretend to be still asleep, to fall back into the comfort of the sheets, which belong to Sissy. Always before, Sissy has been far away, and Wendy is supposed to be asleep.

Leon is naked and tall. He is holding his cock in his hand, tentatively, and now he strokes her hair. His eyes are brilliantly coked-up.

"Where's Sissy?"

"You know what people want?" Leon says.

"No."

"The king," he says. "They all want to be the king."

"Leon," she says. "Where's your wife?"

"We were in LA, at the airport, and I was looking right at her. There were all these people with their tickets. Waiting in line. Fighting at the counter. All these ugly people with their tickets and their Walkmans and then I saw her. I was looking right at her. We were in the airport and then I knew she was lost without me."

"Okay," she says, nodding. "But why do you want her to find out?"

"We've been married all my life," Leon says. "This is about you."

"I thought you did this with everyone. You being the king and whatnot."

"If you catch a falling star," Leon says, "you burn right up."

It's the first time they've ever talked about it. Later, she imagines she is somewhere near Jamaica. She is standing waist-deep in the water, which is blue and full of stardust, and she is waiting for the waves to break. The water is warm as semen, and eventually the sky is full of stars, falling, one and then another, burning across the sky, and she can feel her hair in the breeze; she can feel the end of the day, caught in her throat. She can feel Leon, giving up, beginning to recede. What happens to a man when he cannot find the shore? It is important to know the sea is never full. The sea, like the sun, always rises, even if it is entirely our fault. What is needed now is silence: because somewhere, down a hallway, a good friend is waiting by herself. Unable to breathe, it is impossible for her to come. Then the semen lingers on her collarbone and throat. The body of evidence, which is nothing more than a vague remark you learn to leave a while before waving it aside.

Sin is more easily justified than existence. One steals because one is often hungry—as in Newark, or Somalia, or all those people watching television all alone. And when two become one, she thinks the other half of each must surely die. Looking out the window, she understands the shape of things to come: there are those who do, and those who do not. A house divided cannot stand. A DJ is neither a musician nor a priest. If she wanted to play an instrument, then she should have taken lessons. Leon, the Rock Star, taught himself to play guitar, and later the piano, just like Elvis. Certain critics who cannot play guitar often admire his technique, though they are always quick to mention that he is, nonetheless, unschooled. At school one learns the rules. One learns to play fair and pay attention. *To choose is to be,* wrote John Donne, among other things. *But to be a part of nobody is to be nothing.*

If she returns to Paul, in New York City, then clearly she will belong to something: marriage, that great institution of economy and deceit. Soon they will be buying cards for one another at Hallmark. *For a dutiful wife, a dissolute husband* . . . the script all loopy and polite. All in all, a thriving industry. She once told Paul if he didn't check himself into an institution, then somebody else was going to have to. His lover, his boss—sooner or later, people were going to be quick to agree.

"It's all in the mind," Paul said, dismissing her. "Thinking makes it so."

If such things are still possible, then she wants to be full of light. God is light, like a feather, or a shaft. In the desert people often die of sunstroke, and it's the kind of thing she always did alone. She'd set out a few candles, giving herself up to the entire day. Take a little in, give a little back. Tit for tat. And even now the experience still lingers in the mind, especially on her darker days, because now she has her body under her control. Years ago her counselor spent a lot of time listening to her, and in the hospital, somebody decided that she did not want to die. She wanted to be light, like God, yes, and she wanted to make herself feel good . . . *certainly* . . . but she was willing to agree she did not want to die. Years later at a radio station in the center of the night, sipping at her iced water, she often wonders if she's healthy. Probably she is just looking for a better way to disappear.

On the air, you cannot see the voices coming to you, but you can always feel them coming. Last summer, with Paul, in Leon and Sissy's pool, he had whispered to her in the water. He had put his arms around her and lifted her from the water. The entire visit, he drank only water and beer. They had the house to themselves, and she imagined one could hear them, inside the house, and out, and then he had to go away. Wendy drove him to the airport. He said he'd call her soon and that he loved her. He said, "Soon we will be all through this."

"I know," she said. They were standing in the airport, which was cold. The carpet was orange and the terminal had multicultural art upon the walls.

"Be good," Paul said, which sometimes meant different things.

"Be careful," she said.

"I'm worried about you. Not me, Wendy. It's my turn to be worried about you."

"I've gained three pounds," she said. "I'm fine."

"That's not what I mean." Paul looked at his watch and said, "We're far away. We get lonely. People get lonely—"

"Do you want me to get tested? I mean, would it make you feel better?"

"People," Paul said. He looked at the people waiting to board the flight. "People are not safe."

"Nothing is safe, Paul. Safety is illusion."

"Wendy, Leon is not safe. If you want to get tested," Paul said, nodding, "I'd like that."

"Okay."

"But there's no point in making it a habit."

"Uh huh."

"The testing," he said. "It gets expensive."

Her great-aunt Angelica died when she was thirty-two. She weighed less than ninety pounds and lived alone on her brother's farm. The move from Memphis turned out to be a blessing in disguise: in Indiana, people dressed a little differently, and there was still a lot of land. It was a place rich in soil. Vegetables grew like weeds, even faster, and in 1893 it was still possible to believe that one could feed the world. Alone in her barn, living with her brother, Angelica never met the man who invented radio. She never even knew his name.

"Wendy," Sissy said, in college. "You can't keep throwing up."

They'd lived together for two years before Sissy finally made her go and see a counselor. Then one night they sat together on a sofa in a common room and wept. Two young girls, crying in a dormitory, and by now they are each familiar with the signs: a symptom is not a cause. In the backyard, Leon is lying on the lawn, his belly tan as rosewood. He's been good for three hours and several minutes, hasn't had a single snort. Sissy is reading on the sofa, and entering the living room, the living room bright with flowers delivered each and every Tuesday, Wendy knows she has been wrong. She knows she has a secret to disclose, and she knows she never will.

"I'm bad," she says to Sissy. "I need to be divorced."

"You're tired," Sissy says, looking up. "You need to quit your job. Why don't we take a trip?"

"Then what?"

"Move away. Tell Paul to follow you someplace nice. If he comes—"

Sissy sits up, puts away her book. She opens up her arms, and this time Wendy runs away. She runs out the door, across the granite lawn, into the driveway. She stands in the driveway on the asphalt, barefoot, and soon her feet begin to burn.

Sissy follows her outside. "Wendy," she says. "Wendy—"

"My name is Angelica," she says. Now she begins to laugh, hysterically, and then she falls down on the driveway. She lies on her back, her thin legs lifting up into the air, and looks into the sun. After a moment, she can't see anything at all.

"Come inside," Sissy says. "Please?"

"No."

"Leon," Sissy says. "Leon is leaving in the morning. I'm kicking him out."

The bride of Christ is taught to love her husband dearly. As for Wendy's father, he disappeared into a glass, darkly, and left behind a woman's diary. Dust to dust—aside from combustion and the microchip, the world really hasn't changed all that much, especially for a woman: she is still expected to want a man she's married to, and not another, or none. Wendy has spent a lot of time figuring it out, and her great-aunt eventually starved herself of company. She lived on a farm in Indiana in a land of make-believe: if you make it, then certainly you must believe in it: corn, and wheat, the value of a hard day's work. As for the man who invented radio, he never got the credit, because somebody beat him to the fair. That is, he simply did not show up first.

Tonight, Paul says he wants a divorce, which means he wants her to fly out to La Guardia tomorrow. Perhaps she could catch a flight with Leon, he says. "Aren't there drugs in New York?"

It is late and she likes to be alone, which she knows is dangerous. She is in the studio, talking to Paul in New York City, which is all the way across the country. It is the kind of conversation which could turn either way, depending.

Now Paul says, sloppily, "What do you think?"

"I'm afraid."

He takes this as a cue. "We are not going to make it," he says, sounding it out. "It's not working anymore."

He is waiting for her to disagree, she knows that. She knows he wants to argue. She could still pack up her life and deliver herself to him early in the morning.

"Wait—" she says. "Is this an ultimatum, Paul? Wait—"

She reaches for the log, checks the clock, punches in a PSA. This one is about condoms and disease. She doesn't want her life to be about disease; she thinks there must be something necessary, something meaningful she still needs to do. She says that now, into the microphone. She says to all the midnight callers, "Life does not have to be an ultimatum, unless you make it one."

She says, "The spirit is willing. To kill a virus, you have to kill the cell, but stone walls do not a prison make. Look, it's still possible to phone home." She says, reaching for her glass, "I'd like to talk about home. If you want to talk about home tonight, give me a call. If you're sad, if you're lonely, give me a call. Give me a call and we'll chat."

"Wendy," Paul says.

"Reach out and touch someone. So to speak."

"Wendy?"

"The cell is the source of life, okay. Fine. We are prisoners to our condition. But what I'd like to know for sure are the conditions. So who out there has got some good ideas?"

She is vaguely aware that Paul will not hang up, though only God knows why. To reject the world is to reject the love of God, but to divorce a man you love is not the same, merely harder. The phone lies on top of the chart, and eventually, to her surprise, the line goes dead.

"Give me a call," she says. "We'll talk. The lines are open now and we are on. "

By now the phones are lighting up. At home, where her friend Sissy lives with Leon, neither is sleeping in each other's arms. Leon is a rock star, and Sissy is a wife who now belongs to Narc Anon. Paul, who lives in New York City, still believes he needs a woman to hold onto, and if she wanted to, then probably she could play another song. She could turn a couple dials, push a button and make some pretty music. She doesn't have to let herself be fired in the morning, though now the board is lit up like the sky, simply irresistible. Hunger, she thinks, has made her realize she is capable of being more. Because at night, before the longing turns to bad, it often feels good for just a while longer. Even alone, sitting all alone at night, working in a studio . . . even alone she knows that she can close her eyes and clasp her hands and feel it in the center of her ribs.

"This is the land," she says. "We have our inheritance."

Why do you feel bad? her counselor often asked.

Why do you feel anything at all?

The idea used to be to make yourself small as possible. Less surface contact, and friction. If she and Sissy take a trip, after packing Leon's suitcase, then maybe they can all plan to meet up in New Orleans for Mardi Gras, or Christmas. Tomorrow, she will have to think about another job, because now it is the morning after, and still her life feels incomplete. Inside there is a big and hollow space, enough to fit the sky, and for the moment she is walking down a city street, the wind in her hair. The street is hot and full of traffic. To the left, the airport is only a few miles away. Madness, she now believes, is just a more efficient means of letting life go right on through you.

Eventually, and as a matter of course, she is startled by a long black car. It's a limo with a sunroof, and the man driving wears a cap. He rolls down a window and asks her if she'd like to step inside.

"Where to?" asks the man.

"I'm not a hooker," she says.

"No," says the man, sadly. "I mean, did your car break?"

Somewhere overhead lingers the morning star, and in the back seat sits a woman with a little girl who is drinking orange juice. The easy choice would be to step inside, to let herself be carried off. Because once, a long time ago, there was a star who fell from grace. He descended into hell, and after a little while he rose again to investigate a garden. Then we learned too much and were compelled to plant our own: we had to develop irrigation, and a wheel, and then we had to make a bill of rights . . . *Thou shalt take the body in order to let it go* . . . because here, in a city just beneath the ozone, it is still possible to try again. It's a song she's often played before, and now she's waiting for the chorus. She's waiting for a woman in a long black car to offer some advice. And she knows she's going to have to carry her own weight. She knows the sky is also full of angels. She knows she'll have to stay a while longer, here on earth, as it often is in heaven.

Because things pass us by, like the speed of light.

Here, Leon had said, falling into her sheets. *Catch.*

Two

Wonderland

Heartache wakes me early in the mornings. Saturdays, when I sleep in, I wake thinking about the day. Maybe I will linger near the window. Maybe I will write another letter. Maybe I will make the bed and think of you.

It's taken me a while, though. Sometimes I go dancing with a divorced man. He is a kind man, short and not very handsome. When I get sad he worries he may be responsible. His ex-wife stays at home and takes care of their children, two girls and a boy. I've seen pictures. The wife is overweight and complains of asthma. My ex-husband is a mail carrier and likes to take walks in the mountains. Hiking, like healthy people.

There's a lot to hike here: the mountains, the woods up near the lake. The canyon still isn't very far away. The weather is often spectacular and unexpected. Just down the valley people are worried about the tourists and the smog. I love the mountains here, and the windows; everything here is lovely just the way we planned. In the mornings, Heartache wakes me early.

I'm back.

After you left I went to Wong's and tried to get myself drunk. I experimented with rum and despair and an orange-flavored carbonated beverage. When you called from Lincoln, I was still sick and said where are you, and you said, "In a blizzard. I'm going to need to use your Visa."

There was a lot of room still left. We'd shared more than that. You said you still had a terrible headache, Heartache was wandering around the kitchen, pissing, and I remember wiping it up with paper towels and then sitting on the floor, crying. I kept crying and Heartache nuzzled me with his wet nose. Since that time, he's been good about letting me know when it's time for him to go.

And I think about that often. His always letting me know. Mornings, he whispers to me in the ear. When one of us has bad dreams, we each wake the other gently. I can't sleep anymore unless he's with me, which is kind of pathetic, a thirty-year-old woman sleeping with a dog. Porno magazines would have a field day with it. A woman and her dog. Once you said to me that men don't like aggressive women, and I said back to you that No, you were wrong. Men just don't like aggressive women they don't want to fuck.

You laughed a lot then, and I realized I had taken you by surprise. Like that time off Lake Mary, in July, when you said, "Oh. Oh Jesus, Mary. Jesus."

Maybe I still can make you blush. Why do we tell each other anything?

My mother believed in Jesus, and Mary; my father said she was usually full of shit. I don't know why my father hated her. His health was failing and I know he missed his garage. Mostly, though, I think he woke up one morning and realized my mother had never been beautiful, and that she was going to die of skin cancer, which wasn't going to help her looks any, and perhaps he was beginning to realize he wasn't ever going to be able to help her. He was beginning to understand our limitations? Each Saturday Mom would go and get her hair done, before the water came, and I'd be out with Dad cleaning out the kennels. We'd load up the honey buckets in his truck and he'd say, "Mary, grow up and be a pretty girl. If you're a pretty girl, you won't be treated like a dog."

That was the summer he was training a dobie for a truck driver. The dobie's name was Mack, as in truck, which was a silly name. Mack was skinny and didn't have any confidence. He was spoiled from his truck driver smacking him around so much. Dad spent a lot of time convincing Mack he should learn to hold his head up. He'd tell me to get on my knees, and to bark and then play dead, and then when Mack started to bark back, I was supposed to wake up and run away. This way, Dad explained, Mack would know who was boss.

I remember thinking it was a lot like the way Mom was around my dad. She'd be a bitch and he'd go outside and check the kennels. That summer we had Mack was when I knew I wasn't ever going to get married and be like my mom and dad. I knew even then some things simply weren't meant to be, like water in the desert, or certain types of flowers. Like the town we lived in, New River, which was mostly a dusty road where the land was once really cheap.

My dad was from Paris, Maine, and he'd make it a point to let you know. He'd say, "Howdy. I'm from Paris. Paris, Maine."

Mom said the first time she thought he might be French.

So why am I telling you all this? Mostly because I want you to know that I knew I wasn't going to get married until I surprised you out at the lake. I had decided we were meant to spend our lives together. I remember you calling out my name and me being unsure if this was the way you did it properly. I mean, I'd read about it in books, and in Dad's porno magazines, but I'd never really put one in my mouth. I remember too the way it felt, inside there, and being worried I might hurt you. I remember thinking I could really hurt you, and that I loved you because now I could hurt you so very badly. I swear to God I could taste it even then. I mean I loved you, Joseph. I mean I thought of you, and me, and what our names meant. I thought, *God is love.*

Then I worried you'd think I did it all the time. You put your hands on my head and I pulled back my hair so you could see what it looked like. Because I wanted you to know everything even if it meant that I was clumsy. Outside the sky was blue and I could feel the grass beneath the blanket, and then there we were, beneath the sky, and I thought, *Yes. Yes this is what it means.*

Did you know then what this meant?

Of course not. You thought I was a pretty white girl who could teach you things about yourself. Odd and interesting things you just happened to come across while straying through another world. Doesn't this surprise you any? You thought I was an aggressive woman. Having grown up some, I will never understand why you are so afraid to use your mouth.

I know, a cultural thing. One thing I have never been is too aggressive. I remember thinking after you called me from Nebraska that I should really be more demanding. I thought demanding people get what they deserve. I mean, I was a good person, I meant well, I deserved better than this. Instead I called my dad. There was a new litter of pups, he said. The runt was still available. Mom was moving out but Gracie was doing just fine.

Growing up in a kennel, you learn about biology differently than most kids. My dad used to say dogs lick themselves because they can. I mean, at nine years old I was watching Gracie take a stud. She was Dad's biggest treat, all liver and white; later, he'd show her all the way in Lexington. Mom was just starting to get into Danes, which Dad said was silly. He said, "The old lady just likes a big piece of meat."

I knew what he meant. The first time I watched, it hurt inside. I mean, there they were, all goofy and naked looking, and then after, after they locked up, they just turned and stared away at us embarrassed. I know dogs aren't usually embarrassed, they'll take a dump in front of anyone; I'm not into anthropomorphizing pets, at least excessively, but Gracie was definitely embarrassed. She had this big stud inside her, trying to get out, and instead they were locked up tighter than a drum. A heartbeat, and then another, and even then it was pretty clear who wanted to leave whom. Dad was holding Gracie's head, and then he said, "Mary. Mary come here."

"What?"

"Take his head," he said.

"Okay."

"He's finished," Dad said. "He wants to go. But he's too swollen up. When a dog finishes inside a bitch he gets too swollen to go away. They get locked into each other. It's the way dogs get married."

"Married," I said.

"Yep. Married. For a dog, it usually last seven minutes. Give or take a few."

"He looks sad," I said. "He looks like he wants to go away."

I showed dogs and horses all through high school. We didn't have any running water inside the house, or a television, and during the summers it was always hot, but we had a lot of animals to work with—just like the beginning, with Adam and everybody else. Sometimes I'd pretend I was Eve, or someone even more beautiful, conceived by something more than just a bone. My parents may have hated each other publicly, but they always bought me books. Sometimes Dad still worked on a crippled airplane behind the kennel. He said he missed the grease, and he taught me about the parts of engines. Things like gaskets and fuel lines.

The bus to school took over an hour. Actually it was a small, yellow van, and I'd go to school smelling like a barn yard. Boys made fun of the way I looked, and my boots, and the way I never had clean hair. In the hallways, boys wouldn't look at me and girls would stop talking and sniff their noses. In Phoenix it wasn't fashionable to be a cowboy unless you were a tourist and didn't know any better. I never thought of myself as a cowboy, or girl, until people started calling me a shitkicker. We were supposed to be ugly and not know how to get along with people who wore pretty clothes. Our jeans were never quite as expensive as the kids' from Michigan and New Jersey.

I was a shy girl, you see. I was smart, and going to get a scholarship to a fancy college, just like you—a private meeting of two separate minds, off in Connecticut. Naturally, I knew a lot about geography and foreign languages, but I wasn't used to doing all those things. I mean, okay, I rode my horse, often bareback, and I knew all about biology. My mom wanted me to be a veterinarian and Dad said a girl should travel if she wanted to see the world. Once, he sold magazines across the country and learned to hustle pool. He'd talk all about the way he was really from Paris. Like I said, we didn't have a TV, which made it easier to pretend that we were happy, so I went away to college and fell in love with an idea of you. And after Mom left to live with her sister in Jacksonville, who had married a black man named Mr. Washington, Dad said he was going to sell the kennel. He was going to see Gracie through one more litter before he sold the farm to a developer.

It was a different bitch, of course. This was Gracie number three.

Burns and Allen, that kind.

My mother is dying in Florida of skin cancer, and you called me from Lincoln and had to use the Visa. You still had a headache, and partly it was a relief to know I didn't need to stay in Phoenix waiting for you to change your mind. I packed up our things and then threw most of yours out. Your letters, your underwear and socks. There were all those stupid cans of soup still left inside the cupboard. I packed up the car and left the valley, crying, and drove up here into the mountains. Now I'm living in a trailer on the edge of town. There's a big field outside for Heartache to play in. When it snows, he looks all around the world, each time a little bit more dazed. There's so much up here to take in daily. There are a couple people in town I train dogs for. I teach the dogs to sit, to stay. I teach them to be polite, to behave not quite naturally in order to get along better in this life.

The flesh, it belongs to all of us, and I have new friends now. I have a dog. I have a lover who brings me my mail on time and pays his child support punctually, and when you say that you can change the world, Joseph, I hate you, and then I hate myself for the way it makes me feel. Hatred, and what that great place is still capable of doing to me.

The dog is the descendent of the wolf, which is why dogs prefer to live in packs; they each carry their history with them, deep in the blood, adding a little bit more with each passing generation: how to flush big birds, how to scatter sheep away from foxes, how to howl at the moon. Since the beginning of time, they have been genetically instructed to live in groups and sleep together. They have been bred in the bone to rely on the one true source of heat.

Just because I lived with you doesn't mean we knew what we were doing. Once we made love nearby a lake during Christmas vacation, but that doesn't make life easier. You didn't know I'd changed my mind, that it didn't matter to me if people wouldn't wait on us in restaurants. I wanted to raise a family and instead you left me, and I went to a bar, and then a couple hundred miles later a man with three kids asked me if I'd like to dance. Imagine that, me, suddenly being popular. First comes love, then comes loss. I suspect there are other things that come between. A dog learns to sing because she's lonely.

It becomes the call of the wild. When Aunt Jean brought

out her new husband to visit, my mom was all excited. She picked wild flowers and put them in a Coke bottle. She made Dad fix the front gate and go into town for ice. And then Aunt Jean drove up the road and stepped out of her rented car with a black man named Mr. Washington.

He was short and skinny, like Dad. He was smoking a cigarette and looked all around at the sky. It was July, which meant it was at least over a hundred and ten. In Jacksonville, it could be hot in the summer, he explained, but not like this.

And then Mom did a peculiar thing. She went through the gate and up to Mr. Washington and kissed him on the mouth, as if he really wanted her to. She said, "I'm glad to see Jean finally got some sense into her head. Welcome to Wonderland!"

In Phoenix, and though I was now probably nine or ten, I still had never seen a black man. I grew up thinking it had something to do with the sun. Also, I didn't know people still alive might think there was anything really wrong with marrying a black man.

Then my dad called Mack, who came to the fence hard, stopped, turned around and then took a flying leap right on over it. Mack danced in circles, snipping and yapping all around us until Dad dropped him at Mr. Washington's feet.

"Mr. Washington," Dad said. "How d'you like dogs?"

It was the first time I ever saw terror in a man's face. The second time I so vividly recall was when you told me you were leaving. You stood in the kitchen and said you were leaving me, that you had to get on with your life, as if living with me for six years had meant it had merely stopped. As if it meant that together we did not have a life together that was also yours. As if everything between us was merely frozen and scared stiff.

But Mr. Washington did a brave thing. He kissed my mom back, in front of Dad, and then he reached out to pet Mack.

His hand was shaking, and sweaty, even on the top, but he petted Mack nonetheless.

He was considered family from then on.

I wonder sometimes who it was that taught us how to live. I don't mean tying shoes or brushing our teeth. I mean things like fire, and ice. I mean things like love.

That's what work is for, I know. In Flagstaff, seven thousand feet above sea level, the air is thin and full of wood smoke, and each day here we are visited by the Santa Fe. It doesn't matter where you are in town, you can always hear the train blowing its horn; we are relieved, and thankful for having it come across so great a distance. Gallup, and before that, other places. The trains are always full and long, and all around town, you can see peoples' eyes light up. Suddenly, it's easier to straighten up your hair, to scrape off the mud from your boots. My mailman likes to go sit on the side of a steep hill and wave as they come by. Sometimes he invites me to come along.

"Freight," I might say, looking up.

"Mm hmm. Lots of it."

And then maybe we'll get up and play with my dog. We'll throw a stick for a while. At home, each night before we eat, I always check his paws for burrs and ticks.

Sometimes I call my mailman my ex-husband, though he is not *my* ex-husband. Once, during an argument, you admonished me for failing to provide a solution to the problem of loss, as if it were in fact my responsibility. Now, because I know more than I used to, I suppose it is.

My dad told me once he was jumped by a bunch of blacks in the army, which is why he had two teeth that didn't belong to him in quite the way God intended. He said they jumped him because he was white and skinny, and because he was walking down a dark street all by himself. He said it was his own fault. At first, he was considered AWOL. He said he spent a lot of time in this life hating black men.

But Dad and Mr. Washington got along real well. Dad liked showing a man around the place. Together they poured a cement floor for two new runs, and they talked about plumbing, and maybe getting hot and cold water someday. There were always a lot of chores to do.

Once Mr. Washington said to Dad, "Bill, are you French?"

They were sitting on a bench, smoking. Dad said, "Naw. From Maine, actually."

And then I climbed up on Mr. Washington's lap, and he and Dad had conversation, and after a while I could feel it underneath me. You know? I could feel it even then. It belonged to a man, and it was rising, and then Mr. Washington lifted me up like a little girl and set me on the bench beside him.

"You're too big a girl for that," he said, nicely.

I didn't know precisely yet what was wrong, but I did know it was something unintended, and that he was nonetheless ashamed.

So when you told me you had to leave, I think I already knew it was because you were ashamed. Sometimes I wish you believed in us the way you believe in future generations, in justice, in the brotherhood of man. By man you always mean the Black Man. You don't mean men and women. You don't mean *everybody*. The institution is a source of power, regardless of whose, and power by its very nature wants merely to be expressed—if it's not poor kids in the barrio, it's rich white women pressed up against the glass ceiling: sooner or later, we are all going to explode. Then again, without Cain and Abel, we wouldn't have a history for Christ to come along and remedy. When my ex-husband comes over to my trailer, I often say to him, "Deliver me. Please."

It's become our private joke. We have other private

jokes, things you don't want to hear. It's important for you to know that we can learn to love another deeply as our convictions. Monogamy is a misunderstood idea too big for most of us to grasp: I love you; you love me; let's not think about the rest of the world too much just yet, because it's complicated.

And not likely to change very much over the course of the next hundred years—space ships or not. What I'm saying, Joseph, is that it is possible to love the world and a woman too, even if she is of another race. Among the faithful, slow and steady always wins. Slow, and steady, the way we taught ourselves to love. Remember? Remember then that some things didn't matter? There was the sky, and there were our two bodies, and the way they introduced each other pressed up so tight together.

Don't you remember Sputnik? And Apollo?

Each day the sun comes up, and I have made new resolutions. I have decided never to keep a secret, nor tell one either. I have decided always to try and say precisely what I mean. To be kind to myself, and to try and love others the way I love my dog—because he wants me to. I have decided that my dog has a soul, perhaps larger than even my own, and I hope someday if our roles become reversed that he will forgive me for my moments of unkindness here on earth. If you saw him, playing in the field, chasing after rabbits and squirrels, it would make your heart leap. You can learn a lot by living with a dog.

They are inquisitive; they believe in watching over their young; they like to play. Chase, and Tag, and Fetch. It's amazing the rules they make up in order to preserve a game. I have other rules, too: to tell people I love them when I do; to count my blessings even when I'm lonely; to prepare well-balanced meals and to remember to take my walks. Bingo, Thursday nights. Late at night, when Heartache nuzzles up to me, sneaking onto the pillow, I put my hand along his ribs and feel his heartbeat, and I know that I am blessed.

I learned to believe in these things from my family, though I never knew it growing up. My mom was bitter and my father was lonely and also bitter. He never had a son. He never made a lot of money. But together they told me to love the world, and for that, Joseph, I am grateful.

You know, I could have named my dog lots of things. I could have named him Fido, or Excedrin. I almost thought I'd call him Your Fault, but then I realized it wasn't quite so simple. He was sitting in a pen, looking at the edges, which used to be full of all his brothers and sisters. There he was, sitting in a pen all by himself, like my father, and maybe you, in some distant office, and then I remembered all over what it felt like to have somebody go away even when you know he needs to.

Then I made up my mind, just like that.

One night, when I was still just a little girl, I was awakened by my mother. I didn't know it was she. I heard only this voice, which I would later recognize as belonging to a woman, and I followed that voice down the hallway to my parents' bedroom. The door was still ajar, and I stood on tiptoe in my gown; it was winter, and I could feel the cold rising from the floorboards. My mother was naked, of course. She was astride a man and calling out to God. She was calling out to God, and I had come to see if anybody was going to pay attention. You have to remember, I was just a little girl, but when I think of all the mean things my parents said to each other, back and forth, again and again, I always think of that night I couldn't sleep. That night when I crept into the doorway of my parents' bedroom and stood waiting for my father to open up his eyes and recognize me.

When I visited him to pick up Heartache, he was sitting alone in the kitchen. He was drinking Coke and chain-smoking and looking at the radio, which had long since been turned off. The dogs all started barking when I drove up the road, and he didn't come out to greet me. Instead, he sat waiting in the kitchen.

"Dad?" I called.

When I stepped inside the house, I remembered that my mother didn't live here anymore. She was moving to Jacksonville, Florida, with her Danes. Even if I was older, the house seemed bigger to me now.

He asked about you, my dad. He said, "Where's Joe?"

And then I started crying, and he put his skinny hand on the top of my head, and said, "There. There."

Eventually the truck driver showed up and paid my father eleven hundred dollars for teaching Mack to bite on command. *Sic,* as they say, and there was one big chore left to do that summer. Mr. Washington and my dad were smoking, talking about their lives, and what they'd once planned to do with them, and then my dad said, "Mr. Washington, s'pose you want to help me with one more little thing?"

"Surely, Bill," said Mr. Washington.

I followed them into the shed. There was a big sign there that my dad had spent the past couple of weeks on: it was white, with fine lettering that said, *Wonderland Kennels.* There was a dictionary on the workbench, because my dad wanted to make sure he got the spelling right. It was supposed to be a surprise for my mom.

We loaded the sign onto the back of the truck and drove out to the front of the road with the cement mixer clanging behind. Dad and Mr. Washington took turns digging the holes, each showing off for the other, just a little, and then I set the sign inside the clean holes. Driving down the highway, on your way to I-17, to Flagstaff or Prescott, or the Canyon, you'd be able to see it big as day. This was Carefree Highway, and my dad was going to establish the biggest kennel in all the Valley of the Sun. After Mr. Washington poured the cement, I brought out Cokes, and then we all stood back, admiring the new sign and all the business and good luck it was going to bring to us.

"Looks awfully nice, Bill," Mr. Washington said.

"Yep," said Dad. "The old lady, that ought to please her plenty."

"I like it," I said. "Now people will know exactly where I live."

We are still so far away. I don't think Dad ever knew that Mom was going to leave him: too much silence can make it difficult to listen; if they had only loved each other, the way I know they always did, then maybe he wouldn't be so lonely now. And maybe she, too: living in Jacksonville, Florida, relying on her Medicaid and her sister and her sister's husband. The skin grafts are painful and expensive. Sometimes people forget to take care of what already belongs to them, and then what's left for anybody else to show?

A chance to speak your piece on MSNBC. A new hairdo to match your melanoma. A letter in the mail from someone who still loves you. You can march in DC all you like, I am always going to be a white girl who grew up in a place without running water. You don't have to make a lot of money to believe in what you know, and if you came back to me, I might not even be here. What I'm saying, Joseph, is that I have my own life, and I am hoping that someday you will no longer be quite so big a part of it.

In Arizona, where I live, you can find yourself caught between two rails. The rails are durable and stretch into the horizon on a bed of gravel; they are tied up neatly with heavy sticks and nails. Soon we will all be laid to rest, but somebody had to put it all together, to teach us to transport ourselves from one place to another. Even in the middle of nowhere, it is still possible to remember who you are, and when I call Heartache, he always comes to me. Sometimes my mailman calls to him, too, though it is clear I am the mistress. I'm the one who takes off the leash. And maybe we'll be outside, hiking. Maybe we'll be waiting for the train. And if someday you come riding by, then maybe you will see us—and my dog, all legs and floppy ears, running in circles all around us like a song. A dog sings because she's lonely, I know this now. It's a call for others to come join her. First comes love, then comes loss. And what follows always is a chance to go outside, wander down the drive, and check the mail.

"Heartache," says my mailman, my ex-husband. "Hey!"

And then maybe I'll join in, because I know better what I'm doing. Because maybe I have decided it is still possible.

"Heartache," I'll call, holding out my hand. "Heartache come."

Insomnia

He thinks about the water often: sitting in traffic; in a chair in his office; in bed with his wife, Jeanette, who is now asleep. Together they live the life of the city, Phoenix, where the smog blisters the horizon and the swimming pools are treated by experts. Byron, his brother-in-law, runs a pool cleaning business. Byron drives from home to home in his sky-blue pickup truck, *Byron's Pool Service,* measuring the pH, the need for chlorine and acid treatments. He has recently hired two graduates from Tempe, has bought each a truck and supplies; next year, he'll be hiring another, business is swell. The college graduates are tan and one of them, the blonde, deals cocaine.

"It's a great job for a kid," Byron said, earlier this afternoon in the driveway. He stood in the sun, his long arms resting on the roof of his truck. "You drive around a lot. You get to listen to the radio, get a tan. And get laid by all those lonesome housewives."

"That's a myth," Tom said.

"Myth my ass. Just ask old snowhead next time he comes by. Ask him if *he's* getting any."

"Drug dealers," Tom said. "It's not the same."

"Kids," Byron said. "Kids. You ask Jeanette sometime. Sometime when you're feeling lonesome. Kids these days— they're like bunnies. Like bunnies and monkeys," he said, wagging his finger. "I'll give 'em this, though. You can't call 'em lazy. They just ain't lazy."

"It's the nature of the drug," Tom said, and he knows Byron thinks he's lazy. All accountants, according to Byron, are lazy. Ever since the calculator. Byron resents him his wife, Byron's sister. At thirty she's still a vision—all skin and hair, and now while she sleeps beside him, while Tom watches the clock, the luminous patterns which read *3:37*, he thinks about Jeanette sitting outside in the sun, drinking her iced tea, reading a book and watching the pool man. The pool man is just a kid skimming orange blossoms across the surface of the water—the pole in his hand a sword. A foil, he thinks. The kind you have to point with to do any real damage.

Since the advent of the repeating rifle, nicotine, like other drugs, has become decreasingly popular. When he smoked he would handle his cigarette like a pointer—a hot, burning tip, punctuating the rhythm of his sentences and ideas. And while he still carries his cigarettes, he no longer smokes them: not for three months. To celebrate the event, 17 March, he picked Jeanette up at the library and drove to the airport. There they caught the first flight leaving for St. Louis.

To quit smoking he had to face his addiction. Whenever he felt the urge, the first shivers of nicotine withdrawal, he would put a cigarette in front of him. He would focus on the cigarette until the shiver passed and he began to think about something else. If he could think about something else, then he didn't want a cigarette. Even at dinner, over his coffee, which he kept, and his Scotch, which he also kept—even then he would reach into his pocket and remove a cigarette, and set it before him, standing end-up. He became less conversational and more stoic. "No one," he would argue, "wants to be an addict. You name me one who does. A drunk, a junkie—a Twinkie nut. I don't care what he's using, no one wants to be an addict," and then he would stop talking, focus on his cigarette, a monument of self-discipline, and feel stronger about himself than ever before. "Just one," he might say. "Just one," and by now he knew that he was beyond the danger of addiction, that addiction was something you need not be afraid of if you faced up to it. He was smart enough to know he didn't want just one.

This is what he thought about on the plane, non-smoking, a window seat where he sat holding his wife's hand. He had smoked a particular brand of cigarettes, one which advertised cowboys and wild horses; Jeanette told him for the first time in years he smelled really nice.

Once in St. Louis they rented a car, found a motel near the airport and bought a bottle of Jameson's. It was, after all, St. Patty's. They drank whiskey from plastic cups and watched television until he passed out. In the early morning, he woke to find Jeanette sitting on a vinyl chair, staring out the window. She sat watching the lights and the planes land, which he pictured as he closed his eyes, turning into his pillow, the planes falling into his mind—the edges blurred by the light on their wings.

"They're so pretty," she might have said.

In the morning, dressed, she did say, "I want to see the Arch."

"I don't want a cigarette."

"Yes you do."

"You're right," he said, flexing, reaching for the Tylenol. "I want to see the Arch."

She had been raised in St. Louis. "When I was a kid," she told him, "they were building the thing. To celebrate Jefferson. The Louisiana Purchase. They kept building it and every weekend we'd drive downtown to watch the progress. And then Dad got a job in Detroit, and we moved. They still hadn't connected the top—it wasn't complete. I want to see it complete," she said, and he had promised someday they would, and now they were in St. Louis and this was something he was remembering: their vacation, on Oahu, the place of his birth. They had married in Phoenix and flown across the ocean and set themselves up for two weeks in a condo which belonged to friends of his parents. Normally, the friends got three grand a month for it, but his parents knew people, it was a small island, and it was then, while treading water in the Pacific, that she told him about St. Louis, and the Arch she never saw complete, and the way when you looked up at the Arch it always looked the same. What was different, she explained, was the sky, and he felt himself drifting on the water, wondering what it would be like if the sky never changed, if only the things below it changed, like trees. Like plants and all those people who planted them and all this water.

Because he cannot sleep, and because he does not want to think about not sleeping, he decides it is time. He rises from the bed and walks through the dark halls of his house; in the kitchen, he reaches under the sink, where he knows there is a half-bottle of gin, a gallon of Chablis, and a full liter of Scotch. He bought the Scotch last weekend and it is still in its bag. He bought it at a liquor store downtown, off Van Buren, the type that caters to the hookers and johns—cheap beer, soda-pop wine. The whiskey bottles were covered with dust, behind the counter, where a man sat watching a television. Beneath the counter Tom knew the man had a gun, it was that kind of place, and the bottle is still dusty. He rinses it under the tap and locates a glass, his whiskey glass, the one with a picture of the Howard Coleman Library stenciled onto the glass. Once, before, when he used to worry about Jeanette worrying about his drinking, he had tried to quit: he had tried to face it the way he would later face his addiction to nicotine. He'd pour out a glass of beer, or Scotch, and set it down in front of him and stare at it. But while he stared at the glass, he would want what it held, and so he would drink it—smoothly and in one pleasant, lingering rush. Addiction, he reasoned, wasn't addiction when you wanted it. It was need.

In the mornings, Jeanette always took a swim. "You've got a problem," she might tell him, someday, shaking the water from her hair. Maybe reaching for the towel.

"Really?"

Of course it's all in the blood: a treasure to be passed down the genetic line, like blue eyes or hemophilia. In your weakest moments, something to be proud of. Usually, it begins at the elbows, a sudden, nervous little twitch, near the joints, really, on the inside—the tender part. From there it spreads equally up the biceps while the fingers grow nervous and clumsy and the brain, ever on the alert, begins to send signals elsewhere: the gut, the ankles—the hamstrings, even, which tighten up as if being choked: the way you lock in a drill bit, by choking it. By now the brain is foggy, its logic unpredictable, caught in the undertow of need. What once seemed clear is now less so. Your sentences become confused, *post hoc,* and what you're thinking is what, simply, is going to stop you now from going through this one more time?

A swallow, you think. Just enough to swallow yourself full.

After clarity comes love. Sweet, feckless love. Eventually the flesh begins to soften, around the eyes at first, and then the mouth, into the neck and arms and flanks until, one morning over coffee and juice, you realize the flesh you have is not necessarily the flesh you want. Christmas last in Hawaii, with his parents and Jeanette, and Byron, who'd wanted to come along—"What kind of swimming pools they got over there?"—they'd shared a room with Byron, and one night, in bed, Tom had wanted his wife, Jeanette, and she had said, "No, Tom. Byron."

"So?"

"So wait," she said, sleepily. "Wait until morning."

And after a while he had fallen asleep. In the morning, he

walked on the beach in a t-shirt. Byron slept in and woke late to fix eggs. Jeanette went shopping with his mother for a swimsuit in Waikiki, and his father changed the oil in their rental car. But on the beach, in his t-shirt, while walking along the white sand, he came across a couple. The boy was in a wet suit, and the girl, a young girl with short blond hair, lay on her back, the top of her bikini curled loosely in her fist. She lay on her back and smiled up at Tom, as if to say *Morning, Dad,* and he had wanted to tell her to watch out. This was a public beach, the cops patrolled it with helicopters, but instead Tom had looked at the boy, his skin swollen with fine, perfect health, and of course the girl, and then Tom had walked on. He could feel the boy's eyes, following him, and he thought never again would a woman look at him the way he had wanted to look at her—in sweet, gentle admiration. He thought about Jeanette, telling him to wait. To wait until morning.

"You know what I think?" Byron said, later. They were sitting on the porch, drinking beer, watching the birds inside his father's pigeon coop. The coop had burned down once years ago. Neighbors said you could see them flaming, the birds, as they tried to beat out the fire. Some of them escaped into the sky.

"No. What," Tom said.

"I think if a man wants to screw around on his wife, he should let her screw around, too."

"You've never been married."

"I think if a man screws around on his wife, it better be worthwhile. I've seen plenty of those housewives, let me tell you. They sit out there by the pool, wagging their tails. Loyal as God damn pups, Bud. Pups!"

"Never," Tom said. "I've never cheated on Jeanette."

"Meaning? Meaning what, Bud?"

"Meaning, why are we talking about this?"

Just then Tom's father came through the gate, holding a

fan belt, the knuckles of his right hand bloody and skinned. He stumbled through the gate, reached into the cooler for two beers, and stepped slowly into the house.

"If you ask me," Byron said, pointing to Tom's father, "I think you better start keeping an eye on your wife. I think your old man's about half lit."

His father had enjoyed the study of our American heritage and raised homing pigeons. Once his father snuck a dove on a plane and flew to the big island. There, he let the bird go, and by the time he arrived home, flying back on a plane, finding his car in the parking lot, driving over the Puli and arriving home late for supper, there she was, sitting on the coop, roosting. His father would tell the story often.

But now outside on his driveway, under the floodlights, it's time for glory. The basketball is dense, in need of air, and after pumping the ball, filling the yellow-orange ball full of air, he's ready to go. The ball in one hand, the drink in another, Tom forces the net. After the ball goes in, as planned, he turns to face the crowd which he can't see for all the floodlights. Still, he hears it, and he knows it admires his finesse—this basketball player with the lovely wife, Jeanette.

"I had a good coach," he's telling the crowd. "The finest coach in college basketball today, Gene Tummings." He turns to the crowd and waves, sipping from his drink. "Gene," he says, nodding. "Gene, you taught me everything I know."

His next shot from the free-throw line sails onto the roof; he can hear the ball rolling across the length of the house, and what Gene Tummings taught him, specifically, was how to run suicide sprints. Running those sprints had taught Tom how to measure his endurance, how to break through the barrier of pain into the promise of a second wind. Once into the second wind, that wind which emerged from all of this pain, he was invincible. And Jeanette would watch him from the bleachers, running his sprints, and he would be oblivious, running.

"My wife," he tells the crowd, smiling, pointing to where she might be seated. "She's a vision."

Now, setting down his drink on the free-throw line, he looks down the length of the driveway. The mailbox is a hundred yards, easy. As easy as making a dash, which he does, but along the way stumbles into his stride, sliding on his belly into a cholla. When he rises from the pavement he understands that his arm and cheek are full of needles. His belly is going to raspberry, and he can't feel a thing.

"Wait," Jeanette said, in bed with Byron just four feet away. "Wait until morning."

Meaning, Tom thinks, that she knew in the morning Byron would be too caught up in his sleep to notice. Meaning, Tom thinks, that this is the voice of experience. And what he wants to know, here and now, standing in the doorway of their bedroom, watching his wife sleep—what he wants to know is where she learned to wait. Where, and with whom?

Most mornings she preferred to swim naked alone. And naturally Tom had not wanted to wait, and Jeanette had slid under the blanket, receiving him with considered affection. There she labored under the blanket and what he thought about, with Byron next door—next bed, actually . . . what he thought about was what she must look like, there beneath the blanket in the same room with her brother and her lover and all this experience. What he thought about was what this meant, this waiting for morning, which she might as well have done. And later, after Jeanette would rise from the covers, spooning him, later the next morning while Jeanette went into Waikiki looking for a new swimsuit, he would know that she was not going to talk about this. He knew she was going to tuck it into the back of her mind, quietly, the same way she had tucked him into her mouth, waiting for him to either come or fall asleep.

Whence comes this experience? The needles in his face belong to the cholla which grows along the borders of his driveway. In the bathroom, with Jeanette's tweezers, he plucks the needles from his skin. The needles are barbed and he is careful not to break them, but even so they break, still under his skin, his hands large and uncooperative. The roots of these needles will remain lodged in his skin until they begin to fester; he will need to dab at the roots with turpentine, or nail polish, he can't remember which. On the beach, when you ran into a man-of-war, the most immediate cure was urea. You'd ask a friend to piss on you and now, after he takes a leak, he rubs at the blisters along his arm and face. He rubs his hand along the skin of his belly and picks out the small pieces of gravel; sooner or later, things are going to start beginning to hurt. Meanwhile, he stands here, in the doorway, watching his lovely wife sleep.

Wait 'til tomorrow, he's telling himself. *Wait.*

If Gene Tummings had been his father, instead of his coach, Tom might have become someone else, and vice versa. Because he cannot sleep, Jeanette must be sleeping with someone else. Tomorrow things are going to hurt like hell.

But he's sensible enough to know there's a way to put that off; he can't remember where he's put the basketball. The whiskey is on the kitchen table, where it belongs, and he grabs the bottle and glass and returns through the garage to his driveway. Because he can trace the first, faint stirrings of dawn, he decides to turn the floodlights off. The switch is located behind a rake, a three-foot-wide rake he uses Sunday mornings to groom the granite lawn, and when he reaches for the switch, the handle of the rake falls forward, striking him in the face. Pissed, he takes the rake and hurls it across the garage.

The rake bounces off the wall, landing on the hood of his car—a fully restored 1968 Pontiac station wagon. A family car with an enormous engine just beneath the painted hood. In the morning, he will have to check the paint for damage. Above him, propped on the beams of his garage, rests his stepladder.

After he thinks about the basketball long enough, maybe he'll remember where he's put it.

Love is for the timid and the damned; in Phoenix, the water becomes necessary, the whiskey supplies him with regret. What if he had reason to be someone else? His wife, he tells himself, is sleeping with someone else. This much is clear, the ladder is unsteady, his father never taught him how to dribble properly, and as he ascends, bottle in hand, he knows what he is doing. He is climbing onto the roof of his house. Once there, he realizes the need for furniture. He descends, removes a lawn chair from the porch and returns to the ladder, climbing once again. When he swings himself onto the rooftop, the chair swings with, disrupting his balance and swinging him full circle—the chair striking the ladder, the ladder falling slowly. When the ladder finally hits the ground, there is a loud, awkward noise, leaving Tom alone on his roof to consider recent events. Simply put, the ladder has fallen to the ground, and the tar paper is sticky with grit; his father never meant a thing to Gene Tummings; perhaps basketball could have been a way of life. He unfolds the chair by the air-conditioning unit and leans back into his chair. After a while he recognizes the basketball, across the roof, sitting in a puddle of stale water over their bedroom. Jeanette could possibly be sleeping with the pool boy, or maybe someone else he doesn't know. Usually she waits until morning when it is safe. Any minute, he thinks, looking into the sky. Any minute now and the sun is going to break.

In St. Louis, there on the lawn beneath the Arch, St. Patty's Day weekend, he thought never had he seen anything so impossibly big. The ocean was big, but not as big as the sky. The Arch stretched across the sky and, looking up at it, he realized he was no longer looking up at anything. Rather, he was looking down at something larger than himself and his wife combined—the promise of good fortune, a homestead. Land for the taking and enough space for a man to milk his cow. Clearly the possibilities were enormous.

"It's so big," Jeanette said. "It's bigger than I remembered."

The air was brisk, washing over the Arch and the shape it described. They stood on a large, dead lawn, and Jeanette shivered inside her coat.

"A veritable wonder of the world," he said, taking her arm. "Let's go inside."

Inside, underground, with the lawn overhead, and the sky above that, they talked to a woman about tourist attractions—a newly constructed mall, the local riverboat rides. The woman asked if they were on their honeymoon.

"No."

"You're so young. And pretty," she said. "You really should go up inside. You can see the whole city!"

Tom wondered if the woman had ever been on a honeymoon; he felt like a tourist, and realized that he was. A visitor in a foreign land. The Louisiana Purchase, which Tom knew Jefferson had been allowed to make because Napoleon had got his ass kicked in Santo Domingo. Napoleon was on another continent, no longer a threat. His navy locked in ice. A long time ago, before he began training doves, Tom's father had undertaken a correspondence course entitled Our American Heritage. His father had often encouraged Tom to learn from the past and to help him study.

Waiting in line, Tom thought about his father, and cigarettes, his head racing while Jeanette read to him from the brochures. The air was hot and still, museum air, and Tom pretended not to listen. Growing up in Oahu, Tom had learned to hate the tourists. He watched a family from Arkansas, or Missouri, standing before them: three overfed children shoving each other, sucking on their Cokes, their parents standing stiffly, equally overfed and uncomfortable. He wondered what type of car it was that they might drive.

"So why?" Jeanette said.

"Why what?"

"Why now—'68. Why build the thing now?"

In 1968 Tom was watching television and learning to surf. His father was in another detox unit, on the mainland, someplace near Portland, and Tom was made responsible for taking care of the birds; his mother was afraid of lice and she wanted to go back to school. She wanted to protest the Vietnam war, expand her horizons. For the very first time Tom realized that maybe she wanted to leave him.

"It's a symbol," he said to Jeanette. "It makes the future seem bigger than it is."

Tom watched a man standing by an ashtray across the room light up. The man took a drag from his cigarette and, exhaling, blew the smoke away and up into the ceiling.

"You know," Jeanette said, taking his arm and kissing him, briefly, on the neck. "I'm so proud of you."

"Just don't leave me," he said. "Promise."

If he hadn't played basketball in college, taught himself to slam-dunk, Jeanette might have never fallen in love with him. He holds the basketball on his lap, watching the sun rise, thinking the basketball is round and in about the same shape as the world. If it weren't for gravity, he'd keep slipping off, and when he holds the ball up to his finger, he thinks maybe he can still make it spin. He can make the ball spin and balance on the point of his finger, only when he does so, when he gives the ball a spin, it doesn't stay in place. He takes another drink, reaching instinctively for a cigarette. He has a pack of cigarettes in his tool box, on the shelf over the washer-dryer, but even now, were he there, standing in front of the washing machine and looking at his cigarettes, even now he knows he wouldn't smoke one. He has too great a discipline; smoke is a matter of the will. Jeanette, who's sleeping with someone else, is proud of him. The sun is filling up the space on his roof and now, when he spins the basketball on the tip of his finger, the ball remains: facing him, spinning, turning him giddy with relief. He still hasn't lost his touch.

Before his father returned home from the mainland, Tom slipped outside. It was night, and late, and still very warm. He slipped into the backyard in his shorts, all white and lit up by the Hawaiian moon; he slipped into the coop and rearranged the straw. Then he took a match and set the birds aflame. To this day, it remains secret, this source of unexpected fire in his childhood backyard. His father came home later, sober, and wept for days. Sometimes Tom wishes he could tell someone. Sometimes, when he cannot sleep, he stays up thinking about other things he's done. Maybe Jeanette wants to tell him what she's done?

Because when he cannot sleep, she must be sleeping with someone else. Wait, she said. *Wait until morning.* In the morning they rode up through the tunnel of the Arch with the family from Kentucky. The family wasn't from Arkansas or Missouri after all. The family talked nervously in the small space of their car, and Tom had to duck to keep from bumping his head against the low ceiling. He sat silently as the family talked on and the car shifted, corresponding to the angle of their ascent, keeping them level. Next year, the family was going to go to Florida; they'd been planning the trip for years, since the birth of Jimmy Roy, who was too young yet to come along. Jimmy Roy was at home with their in-laws, and back in Phoenix, Byron was taking care of Tom and Jeanette's pool.

Jeanette was smiling at the couple, being polite. "I grew up here," she was saying. "But I've never really seen it."

"That's a shame," said the woman. "That's a real pretty shame."

Briefly, the man reminded Tom of his father. They had the same faces, and Tom realized the man was a drunk. You could see it in his eyes, and he wondered if the woman knew. He wondered if she'd leave him if she knew.

Once at the top, they followed a narrow metal stairway leading to the center of the Arch: the observation room. It was the last section to be installed, the final piece of architecture Jeanette had never seen. And now they were here, all together, standing in its center—an integral part of the construction and design. The metal floor was carpeted, and they could feel the wind buffeting the walls of the Arch. The floor was unsteady and they found themselves leaning uncertainly against a window, looking out over the western frontier, industrialized and full of smoke. They leaned into the view and rested the weight of their bodies against the vibrating monument.

"What I said," Tom said. "Down there. That's not what I meant."

"Tom," said Jeanette, "I'm not going to leave you."

"What I meant was, if you want to leave me, then I want you to. I mean I want you to do what you want."

"I love you."

And standing there, leaning against the window, he knew it was going to be dangerous. Here, where there were no longer any Indians or buffalo. Here where there was only the future and all the wrong ways you could turn, wandering through that space reserved especially for you while you went looking for a river, hoping the water clean. Avoiding disease. It was a place you had to travel into all alone, West, where the land was big enough for a man to get drunk for a living. And if you kept living long enough, the land eventually turned to water. The history you knew you were going to have to go through—even without a lover, or a wife, it was enough to keep a man up at night.

"I feel like I'm falling," he had said. "I feel like I'm falling and I don't know where I'm going to land."

"It's so pretty," she said, taking his hand. "It really is pretty, isn't it?"

"Yes," he said.

"This is the part," she said. "Where I'm standing. This is the part I never saw."

Basketball is a team sport, five men on the court; today a woman is even free to join them; without a coach, you may as well be without a team, which you always are. Alone and on the court, who is there left to judge? By seven, though he doesn't know what time it is, he knows he's in control. He knows things are right and going to be okay. Okay, he tells himself. Everything's going to be okay.

From the roof he sees Jeanette walking through the sliding glass door of their bedroom. She is walking through the door carrying a red towel, preparing to take her morning swim. Each morning she does this before even brushing her teeth; something more than merely habit, he thinks. The way things wake you up like that. Jeanette is walking over the deck, up to the ledge of their pool.

Tom stands and says, "Morning."

"Tom?"

"Nice view, from up here."

"You scared me! What are you doing?"

"I'm watching you. That's what I'm doing. Best to wait until morning, so that's what I'm doing. And watching, of course."

"Come down," she says. "Come on down from there."

"You're beautiful," he says, and looking at his wife, by the pool, he feels an unexpected relief. She loves him. Some people just don't know any better, and looking at her here in the still early dawn, everything is inexplicably clear. He is a man, standing over the roof of his house, looking at his wife, and the pool they have built together. The pool is blue as the sky and full of clean water, and he wonders why he never thought of doing this before. He holds the ball up and lofts it into the pool, where it lands dead center, waiting to be recovered.

"Watch," he says, removing his shorts. After, he almost stands perfectly still, eyeing the distance.

Jeanette lets go the towel and lifts up her arms. "The ladder, Tom. Wait."

"Watch," he says, and looking at the water below, he knows there's no going back. There's only going gracefully and following through.

"Tom!"

"No wait," he says. "This'll be good."

The Last Year of the Soapbox

My father used to tell me how to live. Always pay your taxes. Remember your mother's birthday. Never jump-start a corroded battery. He believed in making things work and trying to avoid explosions.

Before I was born, he did a stint at Studebaker. He owned one gray suit, the same he would be married in, and traveled around the country as a freelance automotive engineer. Eventually he ended up in the northern Midwest, the rust belt, where he met my mother. My father, who had been raised in St. Petersburg, Florida, said it was cold, lonely work: courting a woman in Minnesota. Later, after he became respectable and middle-aged, after he settled in at a mid-sized corporation which specialized in suspension and exhaust, he told me to do what I want.

"You're going to have to work all your life," he told me. "Make sure it's something you enjoy."

At the time, I had just turned seven, and I like things to go fast. A few years ago, before I gave up racing for good, I placed twenty-third at Indy. The year Mark Donahue won, I was a kid hanging out in his pits. My father was showing me the ropes. "If you drive a green car," my father explained, "they'll have to tow you in." Now everyone races a green car, and I drive for WAEC, Western Automotive Engineering Consultants, which I own. We're based in Phoenix and work mostly with prototypes. I do some commercial work on the side.

Today we're doing a shoot in Oak Creek Canyon, down

highway 89A—*Arizona's Scenic Highway,* the sign says. And the premise is easy enough: I drive a forty-five-thousand-dollar black European sedan through the switchbacks. I drive hard but safe, goosing the clutch, avoiding disaster. I brake for two lonesome cows. I pass a green and yellow camper full of grandparents from Iowa on an outside stretch and drive on into town, Sedona, a town full of turquoise, pretty vistas and California license plates. Everyone's staring wide-eyed as I pass through town in my black European sedan. At the three-way, I make a left and drive past the Circle-K to Poco Diablo, a golf and tennis resort stuffed with weeping willows, and by the time I pull up to the entrance, the car has been washed three times; the light is fading; Sandy, the director, is getting cranky; and when I finally get out of the car, it's not me anymore. It's a girl wearing a white dress with legs that'll snap a tie-rod. She's standing by the car near an overflowing fountain. The water is spraying, the bellhop's blushing, the rising music a combination of jazz and new age guitar—and there's this girl, all in white, looking like money and silk.

You want the road, the announcer will say. *The road wants you. This is now.*

It's enough to make you hock your wedding ring, a commercial like that. Anything just to get a down payment and take that girl home and have her whisper in your ear, driving her home while she holds your hand in the warm space between her thighs until, later, when the car sits under your carport, compounding its interest daily, you start feeling spiritually bankrupt. A girl like that's a fine piece of work. "A fine piece of engineering," my father might have said, as if he'd designed the struts himself. "Just look at those knees!" and you know exactly where you want her to put them. You want her to put those knees on your chest, under the full weight of her body, until your breath stops cold.

In Homewood, Illinois, where I grew up, I was a fat kid. Weekly I'd get the crap kicked out of me by boys already developed—the ones with muscles and a thatch of hair sprouting from their loins. To make matters worse, my father had agreed to let my mother name me after her brother who had fallen into a river at the age of three.

"Herbie," my mother would say. "Come home after school." She was afraid if I did not come home after school, I would be picked on. Also, I have since realized, had I not come home from school, my mother would have had no one to talk to: I was the Herbert she never had. We went grocery shopping together. While we had our own washer and dryer, we did laundry at the Highland Laundromat; the basement was too damp, she'd say. She never did read Betty Friedan. Instead, she took me to department stores and bible studies and always, if I ever complained, she'd attack with God on her side. Why was I so ungrateful? Why was I so selfish when I had what Uncle Herbert, that water-logged little three-year-old, never would?

Once, when she was convinced I was using heroin, she explained to me the dangers of syphilis and gonorrhea, diseases so pernicious and vile, she explained, yelling, that if you rubbed your eyes after going to the bathroom, you'd go blind and kill all your children. You'd even give it to your wife when she rubbed at her eyes after you gave it to her.

"Do you want to do that?" she screamed, in the car, where we sat parked in front of the Highland Laundromat. The car smelled like fresh laundry, and I had to go to the bathroom. "Is that what you want? To stick your little penis inside some filthy animal and die in prison?"

"No."

"No! No?! Then what's this!" She held up a pack of Trident sugarless gum, cinnamon, that she'd found in my pockets.

"It's gum," I said. "I'm trying not to be fat."

It was an idea that had never occurred to her; my father had been spending more and more time out of town, in Europe, and California. Most people, especially heroin addicts, chewed gum to cover their breath. My mother had read about it in a magazine. And even today my mother expects me to forgive her these mistakes. She lives in Ocotillo Gardens, where she gets reasonable medical care and writes her memoirs, where I visit with her once a month only if she'll promise not to ask me any questions.

Because I'm Episcopalian, I spend most of each service on my knees. In 1986, at Daytona, I buried a Camaro into the third wall. I broke both knees, a hand, and was in Tucson's burn unit for six months. I have scars over most of my upper body and neck and face. Usually, I wear turtlenecks, except for summer when it's too hot, and in church I pray for the forgiveness of sins, I take communion, and I feel good about the way my knees always ache.

Sandy, the director for the commercial, says she understands. When her husband left, she wanted it to be his fault. "Still," she told me, "I know it's mine."

After the shoot, we're sitting in the bar, Brandy's, drinking tequila sunrises. Hope, not her real name, the girl in white, has changed into a t-shirt and jeans. The film crew is drinking beer, and Hope explains that she changed her name for commercial purposes. She's going to be a television personality.

"What kind?"

"Oh, you know. The kind people have to think about a lot. Like Madonna. Or Bjork."

"Bert," says Sandy. "Let's stay the night."

We both know Sandy's a little drunk; no one spends the night at a place called Poco Diablo without first considering the consequences. From the bar you can see a putting green, marked by a single flag.

"That'd be nice," Hope says.

"Let us be grateful," I say, holding up my drink, "for what we have in hand."

It wasn't until the seventh grade that I learned I could fight back. Tom Soper was picking on me in the locker room.

He'd pissed on me in the showers, and now, by my locker, he was snapping me with his jock. Barry Bloyd and Jimmy Jakel were throwing one of my sneakers back and forth over my head. Jakel was a skinny kid who smoked pot, and he was calling me *Herb the Perv*. I didn't know exactly what a *Perv* was, but I knew Soper had stuck his hand upside Linda Carlisle's sweater in the hall between third and fourth periods. I knew, too, that being a *Perv* couldn't be a very good thing to be. So I pushed him, kind of.

"Look," Soper said. "Herb's getting mad!"

Everyone looked. Barry Bloyd laughed and threw my shoe at me. It hit me in the face and I began to cry.

"What are you going to do, Herb? Punch me?"

"Yeah, Sope," Jakel said. "He's going to punch you!"

Mike Ogata picked up my sneaker and gave it to me. Pierre LeClair, who everyone knew was gay, because he had a French name, told Soper to cut it out.

"Cut it out," Pierre said, his voice unexpectedly deep.

And now everyone looked at Pierre, and Soper cut it out. But Jakel didn't. He punched me in the stomach. He snapped my underwear, and I just stood there. I stood there by the bench while Jakel started slapping my head and I realized that I could punch too. He kept slapping at my head until Soper said, "Cut it out!"

But what I thought was, "No. Don't."

Every now and then, Sandy and I get together. We usually start out over dinner, talking about her divorce, and her husband, Wayne, who left her for an actress. In Phoenix there aren't many actresses, most go to Hollywood, but what's important, Sandy explains, is that the girl *wants* to be an actress. The girl has blond hair and does commercials for local car dealers. She has a degree in broadcasting and was a former runner-up for Ms. North Dakota, or Miss North Dakota. Sandy can never remember which.

"Besides," Sandy will say, "I couldn't give him what he wanted."

"Which is?" I ask, politely, if I want the evening to carry on. Each time the answer varies. Sometimes it's *love*. Sometimes it's *excitement*. Sometimes, *me*.

When I don't want the evening to carry on, I talk about my divorce. Everyone but Sandy seems to understand that the best way to shut down an evening is to start talking about old flames.

One night, after dinner, pizza, while my mother was drinking wine in her bedroom, and my father was drinking beer in his garage, I went outside to talk to him. I was in my pajamas and the cement floor was cold.

My father was cleaning a carburetor from an old MG he'd picked up at a junk yard for fifty dollars. He had a cigarette between his lips, his hands were soaked with gas, and I asked him to teach me how to fight.

"What?"

"You're my dad," I said. "If you don't teach me, who will?"

He let out a stream of smoke through his nose, wiped his hands on a rag, and took the cigarette from his lips. He held the cigarette with his thumb and forefinger and pointed it right at me. "What you must understand," he said, "is this."

I waited for him to pick his words. I watched the cigarette in his hand, and now he turned and reached for his glass of beer, his back facing me.

"Your mother will always be right," he said. "You must promise me never to fight with her."

I stood there, watching his back, the way the muscles in his shoulders moved, and realized I'd come to the right place—the garage. And then he turned, facing me, cocking an eyebrow. The glass in his hand was covered with grease, and whenever I want to remember him, I remember that eyebrow, and his eye, looking right through me.

"You'll only lose," he said.

"Okay."

And then he set down his glass. He ruffled my hair and taught me how to make a proper fist.

In college, once while showing off in front of some girls, I broke my roommate's jaw. We had been sparring, showing off, when my roommate popped me in the gut. Pissed, I caught him clean in the chin, snapping his jaw. After taking him to the hospital for x-rays, I drove back to school and moved in with my girlfriend; my roommate had his mouth wired shut, someone said, and he didn't want to live with me anymore. I have also, to the best of my knowledge, done several others damage. I've broken two arms, multiple ribs, and three noses, one of which belonged to that same girlfriend, later my wife, Patty.

I've learned to call them accidents, traffic accidents, and now here I am in a Jacuzzi with Bob, the cameraman; Sandy, the divorcée; and Hope, the rising television personality. The night is black and full of satellites, the air quick as ice. My limbs feel like ghosts, even my knees don't ache, and we're all buck naked except for me because I'm wearing a t-shirt and shorts.

"This is the life," says Bob, who's lighting up a joint. The smoke rises with the steam up into the sky, and I'm thinking this is what happens when you drive the right kind of car.

"Bert," says Sandy. "This is the life."

"I love it," says Hope, who is both stunning and ludicrous. Sometimes her leg brushes up against mine, her skin feels soft as water, and I want to ask her if she really understands what she is doing.

And I know Sandy doesn't really think this is the life. She's been around the block enough times to know this is just a Jacuzzi, full of drunk, lonely people and excessive chlorine. None of this is going to be on tape. After we get out, no one's going to stick it in a VCR. And I know I'll be the first one out, regardless of Hope's thigh, because the steam is thick and making it hard to breathe and tomorrow I've got to visit my mother. It's her birthday. She wants a computer program called WordPerfect.

The way I look at it is this: if we don't do what's right because we want to, then what's the good in it?

I've often wondered what my father thought of me, one of those kids only parents can love: the kind who tries hard, says cute things at the dinner table two, three times a week, and comes home with C's on his report card. As I see it, my father had two choices. He could love me, or he could admit his mistake, which would naturally involve my mother. It was easier to love me and try not to notice my lack of coordination, and on the day I turned fifteen, the same day my mother drove her station wagon with a prototype exhaust to Denver, taking the good china along with, my father signed me up for the Soapbox Derby. He was going to teach me how to race.

"It's all in the design," he told me, tapping my temple. "It begins here."

That was a good year for me. My mother sent postcards from Vail and had a *platonic affair* with her ski instructor, whom she had met at a function entitled *Skiers for God,* and my father began to come home early from work. We'd eat hamburgers and go down to the basement and make plans.

We had to use regulation wheels and axles and a steering mechanism. We had periodic inspections. We dropped thirty pounds of lead into the tail end; weight and gravity, my father explained, work best at the finish. After school I came home and sanded my car, inch by measured inch. I watched the muscles in my arms grow. The car was a layback design, wind resistance was something to be avoided, and in the basement, I'd sit in my car and dream about wind, and driving, and glory. By the time we were finished, the car was a deep blue. "Nothing gaudy," my father said. "Nothing that looks fast. You want to take them by surprise."

Then he asked a draftsman who worked at his company to do the decorating: on the driver's side, in small block letters, my name; and on the other, *Pollution Free Special!* This was, my father explained to the draftsman, to be the last year of the Soapbox Derby.

I won fifth place.

My father died from a series of strokes during my senior year in college. I came home after the first one to argue with my mother and study for finals. I remember getting drunk a lot and standing around in his garage. I went through his tools and found his college diploma beneath a set of Allen wrenches. I found a picture of him and my mother, circa 1957, at the beach. Even in the fifties, people could still be beautiful, and when I returned to Pittsburgh, to that same engineering school my father had attended, I told Patty I wanted to get married. If she didn't want to marry me, fine. But I was going to do it.

"Women don't get married like that anymore," she said. We were sitting at a bar in Shadyside, and she was trying to be nice. "We go to New York," she said. "To Manhattan? We buy stocks and work in tall buildings and visit our lovers in their country houses on the weekend." The way she said that word, *lover,* it was pretty clear she was going to want one someday.

"I want a wife," I said.

"You don't want to feel bad."

Three months later, after graduation, we were married in Connecticut, and I was offered a job for a third-rate team as a mechanic. By December, I was driving my first stock car, and Patty was doing a correspondence MBA. And everything was fine: an entry-level position, a beautiful wife, a manageable amount of debt.

By 1985, we were living in Cleveland, Ohio.

Don't get me wrong, I've been kissed by the best of them—though usually they're wearing a bikini and too much makeup. When I placed second at the Oakland 500, I received a trophy delivered to me by a former Ms. Hawaiian Tropic. She smelled like coconut oil.

I don't think Hope wears coconut oil. Sandy is looking at me longingly, her hand in Bob's lap—you can tell by the look on his face, and I'm just not as good with women as I should be. Hope sits up on the lip of the Jacuzzi now, escaping the steam, and puts her hand on my shoulder.

"This is fun," she says, naked. "I feel like I'm famous."

She starts to giggle and reaches down to kiss me, but I hold her off. I stand, swing her by the armpits over toward Sandy and Bob. Now she's splashing in the water going for Bob because momentum is a hard thing to stop, and I'm up and out reaching for my towel. I'm toweling off in fifty degrees worth of weather. I want to take off my t-shirt because it's cold. Sixty yards to my left is a room with a nice view in the morning and clean sheets. Two hours south, Ocotillo Gardens, and my mother. Patty works for a bank in Newark, she's involved with some important decisions, and I'm smart enough to know I'm getting too old for all of this.

Everyone always wants to touch them—your scars—especially when it's dark, and my mother never did learn to ski. The reason she left on my birthday for Denver was because she was convinced my father was having an *erotic affair*. She was going through his t-shirt drawer, counting his condoms, when she came up with two short. Actually, there were three missing. I know because I took them. I had gone into the backyard, behind the woodshed, and put them on. All three of them like socks in December. I put them on and waited for something to happen until it did. Three days later my mother left, calling my father an *infidel* and *adulterer,* throwing the remaining Trojans at him in the kitchen where he stood drinking his beer, quiet as salt. When she backed her station wagon out of the driveway, the glasspacks chugging like a hot rod, my father said, "Well, I guess she's off to Denver."

Even so, I never told him I was glad that she was gone. And he never told me that he'd had an affair. It was the kind of thing best kept inside of us where it belonged, man to man.

Now I'm wishing he'd told me—the big, scarred kid who didn't learn how to fight until it was too late to do any good. I'm sitting on the edge of my bed, naked and almost content for the first time in months. I'm listening to the springs of some bed on the other side of the wall flex. It's a comforting sound, really. I like to know that people out there, maybe some couple you see in a restaurant ordering orange juice and toast, are the same two you heard the night you couldn't sleep—the night you passed up on Hope, the night of her first break. And the woman's pitch is rising now, an engine winding out. Any moment, I think. Any moment now and that woman's going to explode.

Back before the first war took place on CNN, and before the second war took place on FOX . . . way back when gas prices had bottomed out and people in Texas were swimming in oil, we entered headlong into the age of the fuel-injected V-6. But my father kept his stock inside the carburetor, something you could measure by the throat—home equity, career development, a college education for some kid you happened to let your wife name Herbert. He believed in self-sufficiency and the Alaskan pipeline.

Things which could be easily fixed, I guess. When he was dying, I visited him between strokes. Once, while he could still speak, I asked him why he never became a driver. It was an innocent enough question. The nurses were bringing him lunch, my mother was downstairs looking for a chapel, and the Indy time trials were up on the television.

And then he started crying. I had never seen my father cry, but here he was, staring up at Bobby Unser on the TV and crying.

Later that night I snuck him a beer, and the next morning

he had another heart attack. And then another. He became aphasic, paralyzed, comatose. It was the first time I'd ever heard that word in its proper context, *comatose.* Three days later he was dead.

If I hadn't blown a cam at Indy in '88, I might have placed higher than twenty-third. This was to be the year of my comeback, though I'd never really been anywhere to speak of. Even at thirty, I was still making C's.

Patty was waiting for me in the pits. She was wearing jeans and our team jacket. I peeled off my fire gear and she drove me back to our motel, before the race was over, and then she took me to bed without a word.

In the morning she had to catch a flight to Cleveland—a meeting at her bank. They were going to sell their GSL paper to a servicing company in Jacksonville; Shylocks with secretaries, Patty called them. She stood dressing in front of the mirror—a white blouse, a dark skirt. Her banking attire. She looked at me in the mirror and said, hopefully, "Well, at least it's over."

"There's always next year," I said.

"Why?" she said, spinning around. "Why!" and now she was in tears. She threw her hair brush at me, and then a glass, still wrapped in cellophane. The glass knocked over a lamp.

"You know why."

"No," she said, shaking her head. "No, no, no! Look at you!" she screamed, pointing. "Just look at you!"

And of course she was right. But how do you tell that to someone you love?

So I hit her.

There is one part of the story that never gets told. My mother, when she was yelling at my father, throwing all the condoms at him in the kitchen, calling him an *adulterer,* and *infidel,* while my mother was threatening to leave for Denver, I came down the stairs to listen. I stood in the kitchen door, listening to her scream, knowing that I was responsible and that I could in fact instruct myself to be brave, even if it hurt. Listening, I made up my mind, probably for the very first time. I stepped inside the kitchen between my parents and said, "Mom, I already told you. I took them."

She called me a liar, but I think my father must have already known. Certainly he knew there is no pain like that of a burn, which is pure and inviolable. At the burn unit, I remember Patty standing by me, dressed like an angel—a surgical gown, a white mask to prevent infection. Imagine that: being infected by your wife. Even now the thought makes me wince, makes all the dead skin over my body itch for its ghost.

And this morning, slid under my door is a note, from Sandy: *Taking the Beamer,* it says. *Sorry about last night. Call.* It's typical of Sandy to try and keep things sensible. "It was a fluke," she'll say. "Like my marriage. You know you're the only guy that's ever turned me down?"

Given enough time you can explain anything. As for the morning, it's bright as race day. The willows are green, the birds are singing, and even the coffee is fresh. In the meantime, I drink my coffee and listen to the breeze, and this is what I'm thinking: all over the world, people are doing the same thing.

In 1972, Chevrolet, the official sponsor of the Soapbox Derby, bagged out. Helping kids build cars was no longer an efficient use of corporate dollars: they were retooling for the gas crisis and foreign competition, they were looking into catalytic converters and more economical forms of advertising. And while there were a few scattered attempts afterwards to keep the derby going, the race had lost its momentum. You can only go downhill for so long.

My mother returned from Colorado a month before the big day, in May, when the snow had left all but the highest mountains. She began to go to night school, where she earned a bachelor's degree in English and wrote a long paper on *The Scarlet Letter.* Simply, she had decided to write her life story. Even now, when she's not taking her walks or chatting with the nurses, she's typing away on the laptop I bought her last Christmas. She says it takes a lifetime to figure out what one's done. She's very careful about her pronouns. She wants to get it just right.

So what did I get right? I got in my Pollution Free Special on top of that platform in Homewood, Illinois. I remember looking down at my first rush of speed and thinking this was the greatest day of my life—me in this car, with all these people watching, and knowing, secretly, that the guy on my left didn't have a prayer. My mother had seen to that, and I went up on that block seven times. And when I finally did lose, to a kid thirty pounds fatter than me, I knew I had lost something no one else could. This was my life, and later, this afternoon, when I show up to visit my mother, at Ocotillo Gardens, she'll be waiting in the rec room pretending to be busy. She'll be wearing her new pink dress, her hair will be fresh, and for a while, maybe just for a moment or two, she'll forget about her arthritis and autobiography. She'll see me with candy and flowers and her birthday present, wrapped in newspaper, and then she'll pick at some lint on her sleeve.

"Come over here and sit," she'll say. "You're late."

Radical

Briefly

Her name was Jessica, and in 1976 she is in bed with her lover, James. It is a small bed in a small room in a large college dormitory. Outside the snow is melting, the lawns swollen with muddy snow. Each year, the same things seem to happen, and the days grow warm enough for sweaters, without coats, or boots.

Inside her room on her small bed she is a little drunk; in two hours, it will be time for dinner. James is smiling. Last week she told him she didn't want to see him anymore. And five weeks before that. Still, he's pretty, he says he loves her, the beer has turned warm. She reaches for the beer, still engaged, swallows, and listens to the music. Bartók. Later, when she is living in the Southwest, the college will sell off its art collection in order to pay bills. But before that, and everything else that will happen, someone knocks at her door.

"Who's that?" James says, smiling.

"No one."

Years later, it's a story people laugh at. On Maui, visiting her family, showing off Matthew, the man she lives with, they tell each other's stories. Her parents are very liberal, and somewhere, on the other side of the island, lives her son. He is almost eight, and she has heard about her son only once. She met someone she knew at an airport, who knew the father—a Japanese boy who's now grown up, same as her. Years ago, though. Long enough to have to reconstruct the parts she can't remember clearly.

Her father, meanwhile, says it's good to have her home. She's visiting from the Southwest where she does graduate work in European history, and she is supposed to be looking for a dissertation topic—maybe something about women, something interdisciplinary. Matthew, the man she lives with, listens to the stories and looks out the window at the landscape, at the sky and green mountains. This is his first trip to the island, the first time he's met her parents. Still, they haven't talked about why they seem to be splitting up, however slowly. Matthew is the reason she told James, years ago, before the college sold off its art collection, that she didn't want to see him anymore.

Jacuzzi hopping is one story they tell: she and Matthew, Jody and Al, and a friend of Al's. They started out at the Holiday Inn, on Spence, and worked their way north, up Rural until it turned into Scottsdale Road. By morning, they were at a Sheraton, smoking a joint and taking off their suits. And if she tried real hard, she could tell herself this is what it would be like to be rich: to be able to go anywhere she wanted and sit naked in a warm pool of water, looking up at the sky. The steam rose up from the water and covered the sky.

Years later, caught in the swell of her thirties, she calls Matthew from Chicago. "I need to talk," she says. "I'm flying out."

At the airport she carries a small overnight bag full of silk underwear and socks, a pair of shorts, a new dress from an expensive mail-order outlet. She has never worn the dress before. She thinks the airport is bigger than it used to be, which it is, and they walk quietly through a long parking lot looking for his truck. Then they drive to Tempe, to a bar they used to like when they still lived there. At the bar, she realizes she doesn't know anybody here anymore; only the stools seem familiar. They have a beer and drive to Flagstaff. Today is Matthew's birthday and some friends of his are giving him a party. His boss, and a woman he works with, and a man who's writing a screenplay about Alfred Stieglitz— Matthew has friends now she doesn't even know. Later, he asks her if she can pay for the beer they stop to pick up along the way.

Knowing

Jessica is unfamiliar with Alfred Stieglitz. After James left, when she found the keys outside her door, she realized what had happened. Matthew had come by to return the keys, had heard the music playing, and the bed. College beds make college noise. Red-handed, flushed and otherwise, she had been caught.

It took a long time for things to work out. A year in Sacramento, a shoebox full of letters, Matthew taking a summer job in Minnesota just to clear his head. There he was teaching rich kids to ride horses. He thought about going to France, he wrote. Maybe Greece. Someone he knew wanted to go with, and she knew when he didn't mention her name it was a woman. And she told herself, reading the letter in Sacramento, *This is what it feels like.* Then she went to the library, looking for a quiet place to sit, and eventually Matthew came out to visit, wearing boots and jeans. In Sacramento, he looked like somebody from someplace else, and by September, he was in Tempe, Arizona, doing graduate work. Europe could wait, he said. He might even buy a car. Sometimes, at night, alone in the library, or in bed, she would imagine Matthew standing just outside, listening. Or in a lake in Minnesota, where there were ten thousand lakes, under the moon with a woman who wanted to go to Greece. The moon in Minnesota would fill a lake. In Greece, people could live cheaply and fall in love.

Once, they took a trip, though she can't remember where

exactly. They rented a car. They rented a car with a credit card Matthew borrowed from someone he used to work for, a man who owned a gas station, and they drove the rental car away from the city. On the way to pick up the car, Matthew asked her, "What's the fastest kind of car?"

"I don't know."

"A rental."

It wasn't until after she had rented a few more cars on her own that she understood what he was talking about. Having given up on academe, however interdisciplinary, she worked now for the city and sat on several boards. At Matthew's birthday party, in Flagstaff, Matthew introduced her to his new friends, people he met after coming back from New England. In New England, Matthew taught rich kids to ride horses, and art. He drew a lot of bad landscapes because, he said, in New England there was no such thing as light, or illumination.

Now Matthew lived in Flagstaff where the sky was clear as day. He taught part-time at a university and made less than three hundred dollars a month. Mornings, he cut wood. For his birthday, his boss, a woman with yellow hair, gave him a copy of the *I Ching*. The woman was trying to get him into the university on a full-time one-semester sabbatical replacement. Later, the woman said nice things to Jessica about Matthew. The party lasted a long time, and they decided to find a motel.

"My treat," Jessica said. "Actually, this whole weekend's on me."

"I'm trying," he said, shaking his head. "I'm trying really hard not to be bitter."

That night, in the motel room, she had wanted to take pictures, but she was out of film.

Next day in Matthew's favorite bar, downtown, before noon, they drank a beer. The bar was long and empty except for a few old men on the end sipping coffee. Matthew asked the bartender, a nice woman with gray hair and a falling face, what kind of people came in here this time of day. The men, the woman explained, were drinking bourbon with their coffee.

Later, after the woman walked away to the coffee maker, Jessica said, "I had an abortion."

"Oh."

"Yeah," she said, nodding.

"Does he know?"

Later, in Connecticut

"Get to the root," he said that day in the bar. "You've got to get to the root of it."

"I know."

He finished his beer and looked at the old men in the bar drinking their bourbon and coffee. She took his hand, and he said, "So okay. Okay."

Later he explains he's going to take a summer job in Connecticut, the same place where he taught rich kids to ride horses, and art. Only now he's just going to teach rich kids to ride horses. He's going to have a good time and pay off his plastic. Maybe he'll get a permanent job in Wisconsin.

Three months later, when she flies out to New York, she tells herself she's just going to visit her friends—*their friends*—Jody and Al, who now live in an expensive apartment decorated with pictures of Jesus. The first night, they drink Scotch and talk about the old days, and she decides to give Matthew a call in Connecticut. Rushed, and almost curt, Matthew tells her to take the Brewster North and that he'll pick her up. In the morning, she drinks a cup of coffee and says good-bye to Jody and Al. On her coffee cup is a picture of Jesus, smiling up at her, radiant.

He picks her up, boots and jeans, sunglasses. It's the same truck he had in Arizona, only now there are more dents and one of the headlights is held in place by wire.

"I love him," she says, later, a little drunk in a dormitory room. It's the kind of room where rich kids live when they learn to ride horses, and she's feeling the need to explain. "I moved in with him when the roof fell in. But not anymore. I moved out, Matt."

"I know."

"So what am I supposed to do?"

"I don't know. Make up your mind, maybe."

When she takes off her blouse, he puts his palm between her breasts.

"No," he says, shaking his head. "No."

The next day, in the cafeteria, she sees the woman he's sleeping with. A girl, really, no older than she was in 1976. The girl smiles at her and asks questions about what she does for a living. Eventually, he comes into the cafeteria, boots and jeans, talking with the kids, and she watches the girl stop listening. She watches the girl look at Matthew, and she wants to tell her to watch out.

"He loves me," she wants to say. "It's the way it is. Why else would I be here?"

Instead she finishes her coffee and smiles slowly.

History

James works for an airline at O'Hare Airport. Whenever she leaves town, she wonders about bumping into him in a terminal. He's married now and has three kids, some of whom are boys. At the time, in 1976, the first time she told James she didn't want to see him anymore, she thought she would marry Matthew. She thought maybe they would have kids even. At parties James would pour beer on people and belch. He'd get drunk and pick on a fat kid who wore pink button-down shirts, the kid trying to fit in, using words like *excellent* and *totally* to prove he could, same as anybody. Later, while she was in the Southwest living with Matthew, she learned that the fat kid had washed out of a Ph.D. program somewhere in Florida. The fat kid was also probably in love with her, and she remembers James pouring beer over his head, slapping him on the back of his pink shirt, and yelling, "Schmo! How the hell are you!"

And she remembers hating James for doing that. She remembers fucking him, in her small room, with the radio turned on.

And she thinks she has developed a pattern in her life— that each time she returns home to visit her family, she brings her current lover. James. Matthew. The guy in Chicago Matthew calls Floyd because he knows him from college. Floyd is the man she moved in with after the roof fell in. Usually, the men she brings home are unfamiliar with the ocean, and the water—the way the currents move. Usually, they spend a lot of time staring at the water, and she measures each, looking at the water, making calculations. With Matthew they spent three months, and he didn't have a good time. He didn't get along with her parents. He didn't get any work done. It made her almost want to hate him.

Once, after Mass, they saw the Japanese boy, and her son. Up until then she'd had no idea what he must have looked like.

Still Water

Before she took Matthew home to meet her parents, she miscarried. After Jessica discovered she was pregnant, they had talked about having a baby, and not having a baby, and Matthew never bought a car. She was on her way to the library, riding her bicycle, when it happened.

She realizes now it's not the kind of thing you forget—riding a bicycle, losing a baby. She understands that Matthew must have taken it as a symbol, a sign of things not moving in the right direction. A loss of control. Now, when he calls her up from Wisconsin, they talk for hours.

The department secretary called him out of class because it was an emergency. The secretary drove him to the hospital and he showed up just before they wheeled her in for a D&C. She had already been prepped, she was worried about insurance. About things not working out. Just a week ago, they'd decided to move in together, which they did. They moved into a nice house and told themselves they had the rest of their lives. Not to worry.

On the phone now Matthew says paintings are like babies, only she doesn't understand why. Why paintings are important as babies.

"I'm not saying that," he says. "That's something I'd never say."

"Then why do it?"

"What?"

"Why do it at all?"

And he says, "To make it perfect."

But you can't do that with babies. Paintings last longer, if you put them in storage, and she thinks it's easier to think about what's on the wall, or why you want to put something up there in the first place. Possibly just to cover a stain. She wonders if it's possible to miscarry a painting. To drop it on the sidewalk and watch it die in front of you and then having to go to the hospital, to someplace where the walls are green, to someplace where you permit a doctor with a foreign name to clean out the walls of your interior. She wonders if this is what's happening to him even now. Sometimes, she wants to go back.

Her clock, she tells herself, is simply ticking loudly. She moved in with Floyd when the roof fell in. She was lying in bed, looking up at her ceiling, and it just happened. The plaster fell off the ceiling, falling in sheets; she ducked her head beneath her pillow and thought it was an earthquake. When it was finally over with, she decided not to renew her lease.

Once, in the summer of 1976, she visited Matthew in Minnesota. He took her to the barn where he taught rich kids to
ride horses. He had two horses waiting for them, in the barn,
and he put a bridle on the one for her, and a saddle, and they
led the horses outside into the moonlight. His was a sorrel
mare, which she didn't know until he told her, but she could
tell it was young; it had legs like a girl, she thought, knobby
and long. The air smelled like a barn and he showed her
how to get on her horse. They rode out into a pasture, her
horse following his because she didn't know how to steer it.
When her horse ran, it made her breasts hurt. Matthew said
he had smooth gaits, meaning the horse, and she followed
Matthew under the sky in Minnesota. It was a place she'd
never been before. In front of her, riding slowly, his back
was flat as still water.

More History

In Flagstaff, Arizona, he shared a small apartment with two
people—Deb and Rodney. Rodney had a flap in his brain
which, Rodney explained, was why he couldn't do very well
in school.

Deb was a peroxide blonde and had a boyfriend, Eddy, who
came over at night, usually drunk, usually after Matthew himself had drunk himself to sleep; he'd switched to bourbon
because it was more efficient, requiring less time and money
both. Mornings, he had to be up early to cut wood. During the
afternoons, Deb would struggle with her schoolwork and talk
about her father who lived in Yuma and sold tires. After a
while, Eddy stopped coming over, and Deb started bringing
home men from the bar she worked at. Often, the men were
drunk and Native American—a stumbling cliché. As for Rodney, he lived in the living room on top of a large waterbed
with mirrors; he slept intermittently with two women, sisters,
one of whom was married. He went to the same school at

which Matthew taught part-time on Tuesday and Thursday evenings. Rodney had recently split up with a girl who stabbed him in the thigh with a ballpoint pen.

Deb knew Rodney from group therapy, and Matthew lived in the other room with no furniture where he slept on his sleeping bag—one he had bought years ago, when he thought he was going to go to Greece with a woman from Minnesota. The room smelled like cat piss, from years and years of cats, which sometimes reminded him of a barn. Eventually, sleeping in a room full of cat piss caused him to develop a severe throat infection. He went to the hospital one night, three A.M., and was immediately shot up in the haunch with penicillin. His throat was so swollen he couldn't swallow.

"At all. I mean, I couldn't do it. I couldn't even talk. I thought I had cancer or something. Cost three hundred fifty bucks."

Matthew had no health insurance, penicillin was cheaper than chemotherapy, things could have been worse. Rodney backed into his truck and put out the left headlight which would cost another two or three hundred if he was going to have it fixed properly, which Matthew never did because he knew Rodney didn't have the money to pay for it. One night in March Rodney brought home a woman, the married one, and sprayed her with whip cream. Matthew didn't see this, but he could hear it—the noise the can made when the whip cream came shooting out. And the woman screaming, afterwards.

And then early the next morning, two days before his birthday, she called him up. Matthew stumbled out of his room, into the living room where Rodney slept with the married woman, the sister of someone else he slept with, and answered the phone.

"I need to talk," Jessica said. "I'm flying out."

After he hung up, the woman in the bed turned and rolled.

"Morning," she said, squinting, reaching for a glass of water.

A Long Time

In the end misery truly bores him: while taking place, it offers no real hope, and now when he wakes up in the morning, he tells himself things really aren't that bad. He lives in a nice apartment and makes coffee in the mornings. When he calls her on the phone, from Wisconsin, they talk for hours.

"If I get bitter," he said, back when he was trying hard not to be, "I'll die."

"Don't," she said.

"Okay."

Alfred Stieglitz was Georgia O'Keefe's mentor, as well as her lover and friend. In Flagstaff Jessica and Matthew stayed in a motel so she wouldn't have to breathe the cat piss. In the motel they watched a movie on the television. She bought a fifth of good whiskey, they made love on the sheets, just like television: old lovers, in a motel, making love on the sheets. In the morning she put on her new mail-order dress—cotton, sleeveless and blue. Then they drove to see the Grand Canyon, which was just as big as it was the first time they drove to see it, and the second. The third. Standing there on a ledge, the sun on her arms, she realized they'd known each other for years.

She still didn't have any film for her camera. They stood in front of the canyon and held hands and she said, "I can give you a loan. Really. It's no big deal. Matt, I make a lot of money."

"Borrowing," he said. "It's the only thing that saves us."

"I'm going to move out," she said. "I'm not going to live with him anymore."

"Look," he said, looking at the canyon. "How do you explain it?"

Landmarks

The canyon was finally empty of everything but possibility. In the Jacuzzi at the Holiday Inn, on Spence, the same one they visited years ago uninvited, she looked up at the sky— black as space and full of constellations. Beyond a wall was traffic and she could hear the traffic driving down the street. In the morning she would catch a flight for Chicago. She had work to do on Tuesday and was expected in DC the day after. Upstairs, up on the third floor, they had a room over-looking the pool, and hanging on the back of the bathroom door was her new dress, which she would forget, in the morning, rushed to catch her flight.

In the pool nearby was a group of kids, five or six, drinking beer and sitting on the steps: the girls were young enough to wear bikinis; the boys had short hair, tan legs. The kids were talking loudly, but their voices were unclear, almost distant. Matthew sat on a chair, in boots and his jeans, and she looked up at him and took off her suit. She leaned over the edge and wrung the water out with her hands.

"What?" she said.

"I don't know."

"No. What."

"I guess I just never thought it would turn out this way."

She watched him light a cigarette. He drew on the cigarette and thought about something he wasn't going to try and tell her: that sitting there, in the water, she reminded him of someone he used to know. She reached behind to tie her hair into a knot, and he understood that even the freckles on her chest were the same. Even if they didn't know why, any-body looking would have known they were related. You could tell by the distance they kept between them. By the way they shaped it—like history, and the way it kept mov-ing toward the source of its own making. Somewhere, off in the distance, where there were bound to be some landmarks.

"Take off your boots," she said. "The water's perfect."

Three

Horses

Second-year law. Nights I work at a firm in Scottsdale, ambulance chasers, Goldstein and Kelp. I've never met Kelp, but Goldstein's an alumnus. He tells me to call him Chuck, and each night he's on the tube, wearing a cardigan and contact lenses, telling people he cares. He's telling people he cares and I'm in the files, keeping them straight. I go through two, three hundred a night. Sometimes, I can't believe the things I read.

I live at Uncle Roy's, *Conway Stables,* across the river bottom. Roy gives me a room above the barn and bologna sandwiches, and he expects me to help out when I can. Weekends, mostly. Back in the forties, in Montana, Roy grew up with my dad, and forty years later, one day in March, the air buzzing with blossoms and bees—Roy asks me what I want to be a lawyer for, anyway.

It's a recurrent kind of question. I'm saddling a bay stud, Donovan, who's feeling mean. He smells a mare nearby, and when he turns to take a bite out of my arm, I catch him first. I swing a roundhouse and nail him upside the head. If he were my horse, I wouldn't do this, but he's a lot bigger than me and I haven't seen Kathleen in four weeks. Kathleen lives in LA.

Roy laughs and takes Donovan's head. "He sure do like you," Roy says, still laughing, which is always kind of risky: he's old, and fat, his body's beginning to break up. It's not safe for him to be exerting himself, but still this is something

143

I am good at—working spoiled horses. The farm's about to go bust, some disco wants to buy up all the property, and Roy's daughter, Annie, says she's real glad I'm here. Family. That kind of thing. Roy's got arthritis so bad he can barely walk.

When I was nine, Roy gave me my first hackamore. He and my dad did the town. Later, I left for college. Kathleen went to LA, an MBA, in and out in a year. We were going to go to school together, but I had bad letters, worse grades. Only my LSATs saved me. I got in on probation, and now, when Kathleen comes out to visit, she spreads a blanket on top of the barn; she puts on her bikini and reads her books, and I go off to the corral. Only this weekend, like the past three, Kathleen's not on top of the barn. She's in LA, "in the library," she says on the phone. "You should try it some-time."

She's always been a lot smarter than me, and I know she's hanging out with some guy, Stephen, or Richard—some guy from Berkeley or Boston. He wears tweed and round glasses with purple frames. Last fall in LA, the three of us went to a bar, a hangout, and he ordered white wine. White wine, like he's trying to cut weight.

Roy is saying something to me now, and when I swing up on Donovan, I don't even let him breathe. I spin him tight, once, twice, and straighten him out into a run where I can give him his head. He's finding his stride now and I'm telling myself if he tries anything, even once, I'm going to run him into the ground. I'm going to run his God damn lungs out. I mean, I'm going to kill him.

You've got to remember, I'm just a kid. Twenty-four. As a rule, we do not yet know in America that we are the blessed and correct. When you correct a horse, it often causes pain, and after I finish school, I'll be lucky to make 21K working for Goldstein's brother, Harv, in Tucson. I'll be doing PI with a team of paralegals: college grads who couldn't get into law school—two French majors, a poli science. They'll draft documents on the PC and I'll sign them after I talk with unemployed clients on the phone. All the muddy stuff goes up the ladder, to Harv Goldstein's nephew, Hank. No Perry Mason, no pro bono. Even the nephew doesn't go to court, and later, after a windfall, I'll pay a lot of inheritance tax and go independent. But back then I'm just a hick learning the rules. I've never been to New York or Chicago. I don't wear tweed. When I get dressed up, I wear my Tony Lamas and a pair of jeans. It's the way I was raised.

Paul Newman started out this way, in *The Young Philadelphians.* He worked hard and went to school and fell in love with a rich girl whose parents talked him out of getting married. Kathleen's father owns most of Billings. He says he wants me and Kathleen to come work for him, but everyone knows she's smarter than me. Everyone knows she's going to be wearing the pants. And it's not every day you fall in love with a rich girl who's also smart, who says, sometimes when she's out visiting from California, reading her books on the roof of your uncle's barn, that you're the thing that keeps her going. You're the reason she's so smart. After a while, you've got to try and believe it, or else get smart yourself. Paul Newman got burned. He never got the girl. Still, he's the reason I wanted to be a lawyer, because of the way he handled himself in court.

At Goldstein and Kelp, this case the latest. A guy, rich guy, or at least destined to be rich guy who's now driving a big car, still in his thirties: his name's Powell. J. Adams Powell. And J. Adams is sitting outside on his verandah—actually, a balcony, overlooking the pool at McCormick Ranch: it's Sunday, the Sabbath, and bright as day. The sun's bright, and J. Adams is out with the *Republic,* going through the *Lifestyles,* and probably he's only wearing a pair of shorts. Running shorts, the kind people jog in, maybe, because the guy's in good shape. He's wearing running shorts, sipping his coffee, getting tan on the verandah, and maybe, unconsciously, while reading something about Vanity or Meryl Streep, maybe by accident he scratches at his nuts. You know, just a little itch.

And across the verandah, on this particular day of the Sabbath, is Mrs. Gertrude Simms. She's on her verandah, enjoying the day, and lo and behold, she looks up, and there's J. Adams, that nice boy who smiles sometimes in the parking lot, scratching at his nuts. Mrs. Simms, she doesn't have any nuts, so naturally she can't imagine what it would be like to want to scratch them. And let's face it, not all guys scratch just because they got an itch; sometimes it just feels good, wherein lies the danger. And naturally, there's a scene. The cops come: charge, indecent exposure; specifically, a testicle. *In broad daylight,* Mrs. Simms says, and J. Adams, being the bright guy that he is, he knows he's going to have to do something. He knows it's time to get a lawyer.

When you know it's time to get a lawyer, is how Chuck Goldstein puts it, on the TV, in between the used car commercials and sex ads.

Going through J. Adams's file, I teach myself things about the law. I teach myself things like a man is innocent unless he engages in certain instinctual behaviors upon his balcony; he might have just been eating his lunch, like Mrs. Simms. This thing's going to lay J. Adams back a couple grand, easy, but he's got Chuck Goldstein on the case, and Chuck's the kind of guy who cares. For Christmas, Goldstein gave me fifty bucks cash and dinner for two at Rick's American Cafe.

"Charge it to my account," he said, smiling.

Kathleen couldn't come out that weekend, so I took Annie.

Maybe you don't know, so I'll tell you: most horses are either geldings or mares; that is, boy horses with no nuts, or girl horses. You go rent a saddle horse in the country, that's probably what you get, something docile and safe. But a stud, he's still got his nuts. That's what makes him mean and so worthwhile.

J. Adams is pretty pissed, obviously. He's engaged. He lives a quiet life. Last year, he paid over eighty grand in taxes. This kind of thing doesn't make him feel very comfortable.

"Don't worry," I hear Goldstein say.

"What do you mean?"

"We go to court, we get it expunged."

"How much?"

"We give the judge a laugh," Goldstein says, meaning he takes a ten grand retainer, and then he calls through the office door; he asks me to fetch the file. "Powell," he says, as if I don't know who this guy is. And then to J. Adams, "Want some coffee?"

Later, after the door is shut and both are sipping lukewarm coffee, which I've cooked in the microwave, I'm up front with the receptionist, Allyson. She looks at me, smiling. "Can you believe it?" she asks, referring to J. Adams. "I mean can you even believe it?"

Looking at her, it's pretty clear she wants to believe it: J. Adams is still young, and single; he's the kind of guy a girl like Allyson might want to believe in.

The rest of that afternoon, I'm in the office library, studying. Goldstein knows it's important to me. He gives me chores to do that will help me along. "Go find this case," he'll say, even though he's already got it sitting on his desk at home, or in the back seat of his Audi. This afternoon, I'm studying for exams, reading case after case based on other cases. J. Adams, for all he knows, he's going to be famous: *The Case of the Dangling Testicle, Adams vs. Simms.* Years from now, people could be reading all about it. We're talking about the nature of discretion. We're talking precedents.

"Hey," Allyson says, on her way out. "Don't go blind!"

I say good night and she stands there at the door, smiling,

looking that way she looks, and now she is on her way out: swinging her hips, thinking I'm going to watch, which I do. When I look away, I see Goldstein down the hall, coat in hand, watching the same thing.

I don't say anything. I turn back to my *Constitutional Law* and study the color of the paper. Discretion, I'm thinking. Discretion is nine-tenths of the law.

The law may keep us safe, but it's also what makes us capable of violence: sooner or later, something is bound to break. It's what we have to learn to live with, and three days later, I'm with Annie, riding through the spread chasing off two college kids—a boy and a girl. They're riding mountain bikes, and Roy says mountain bikes are bad for the scenery. Usually, the bikers get pissed off, but we're talking about people wearing pink and green tights, and plastic helmets. They see me and Annie on horseback, they figure maybe they really are trespassing. Also, I try to be polite.

"It's an open range," I say, lying. "You don't want to get hurt."

"Yeah, right," says the boy, aiming for the highway, and we follow along until they get off their bikes to slide them under the barbwire. The girl turns around and flips me the bird, and now we're headed toward the barn. The air is heavy with clouds. Behind us, Papago Park, where we've sent the bikers to, behind us you can see the clouds gathering heat. The creek bed is full of gravel and stones, and Annie says something about Kathleen.

"What?"

"Nothing," she says, checking her cinch. When she leans, her weight in her stirrup, her body leaning along with, you can see her hair falling. Her hair is the color of clean hay, and there is no sun, just the gray swelling sky. Now she takes her seat and turns in the saddle; she looks at me and smiles, briefly. She cues her horse into a lope, and watching her, watching her hair bounce against the flat of her back, I remember something my father might have said. About a woman and a horse. That kind of thing.

Annie, she's just turned nineteen.

Keeping in mind this, too: Kathleen is afraid of horses.

Back at the corral, we sit on the fence and listen to Donovan whinny at the mares. Annie smokes a cigarette, awkwardly, and asks me if I want one. Sometimes, when she's about to say something, she rubs her elbow up against my arm.

"You're just a girl," I say, once.

"That's right," she says. "I'm just a girl. So what?"

My heels are locked in the beam of the fence, and I'm trying to be calm. I can feel the muscles in my arms, reaching behind me for the fence, and I think now would be a good time to tell the story about J. Adams, or something else I know a lot about. I feel the need to talk but instead we watch the sky filling up the river bottom. Donovan is crying, he's bleeding and proud, and when Annie finally leaps off the fence, she half-runs in her boots like a girl. She runs to the gate separating the corrals and swings it open.

Now she's walking back to the fence, suddenly shy, and Donovan is flying through the air behind her. He's flying through the air and Annie's got her fists in her jeans, staring at the small points of her boots. Off in the distance, there's a little Appy mare, pitching her tail, and sooner or later Annie's going to look up at me and smile. She's going to flick her hair and wipe the dust from the seat of her jeans.

It's the kind of thing you have to learn to appreciate, and even then you know it's got the strength to kill you—that Appy mare, nickering in the dusk, pitching her tail.

When I was nineteen, my dad was shoeing a brood mare, Molly O'Brian, who got tired of standing on three legs. He let her go to give her a rest, he stretched his back and lit a smoke, he told me to bring him a trimming knife. But when he turned around, the cigarette still in his mouth, Molly

O'Brian let go with both hooves and caught him square between the eyes. The kick splintered the top of his nose, driving it into his brain, and he died. Molly O'Brian never even knew what hit him. She hobbled over to the water tank.

A horse doesn't apologize for doing what comes naturally; it doesn't need to contend with bloodlines or guilt. If I'd reshod Molly O'Brian the day before, like I was supposed to, I might have never gone off to college. My dad named Molly O'Brian after my mom, who lives with her sister now in Casper, Wyoming. And it's the kind of thing Kathleen could never understand—how I could go to college and leave my mom like that.

As it turns out, Kathleen's making it with Stephen, or Richard, maybe both. She doesn't say this, but she stops calling me up at three A.M. She writes that she's spending more and more time in the library, and that her phone is on the fritz; sometimes, it just doesn't work. In her letters she talks now a lot about internships in New York and Chicago, and she tells me to think about CDs as a way of planning for the future.

In the morning, Thursday, Roy gives me a bologna sandwich. We're sitting at the breakfast table and he leans across for the catsup and winks. His face is full-blooded, the price of bourbon and beer, and his eye's as big as a valve: the kind inside a heart, it's that swollen and big.

"Annie," he says, smiling. "You know she's not adopted."

"Huh?"

"She's mine, all right. She's my own flesh and blood. Same as you, Son."

"I'm not your son."

He sits there, sucking at his teeth, and says, "Yup. You're sure right about that. You're your daddy's son. Thing is, I think of you as if you *were* my son. See what I mean?"

I pour some coffee and Annie gets up and goes to the fridge. She's barefoot and still in her nightie, a t-shirt I never thought she was going to sleep in. I bought it for her in the university bookstore, just a little something, and Annie sets the orange juice on the table. She says to me, "Daddy, he's thinking about his will again."

"Will?"

"I'm not getting younger, you know. The farm's about to go belly-up. You know that. But still, you could put a pretty big house up here. It's not such a bad little piece to inherit. You and Annie, you're family. I want you to get that Goldstein guy to make up my will."

"You'll need to come in, Roy. I'll ask him."

"Jim Dandy," Roy says. "That'll be Jim Dandy."

Roy wants to know if I'm going to marry Kathleen. "Not that it makes no difference," he says. "Just curious."

My dad, while sitting on the porch, looking at my mom walking across the yard, or going into the barn—what my dad used to say was this: "When you go looking for a wife, make sure you watch her ride. Make sure you watch the way she collects her horse." And the way he'd say this, you knew he loved my mom. You knew he'd always known he'd done the right thing, but my dad, and his family and life, were of a dying breed. Now my mom does part-time secretarial work; she lives with her sister, in Casper, and I think there's not much left to say.

So when Roy asks me if I'm going to marry Kathleen, it's not something I have to think very long about, though I wouldn't have known this a week or two earlier. "She's different than me," I say.

We're in the truck, on the way to the office, and Roy's nipping on a flask of bourbon. He feels nervous in his suit, which he must have bought that same year he gave me my first hackamore; even the colors aren't made anymore. He passes me the flask and I fake a belt.

"You mean she's rich?"

"I mean she's bagging some guy named Stephen. Or Richard."

Roy lights up a smoke and says, "California. That's a long way away." He points at the traffic on Scottsdale Road and says, "Shit. When I came here, you'd of thought this place would blow away. If it hadn't been for air conditioning, I tell you. I tell you this place would be a hell of a lot more safe. You could take your kids for walks. Know what I mean?"

"Yeah," I say, nodding.

"Cops," he says, pointing at two cruisers in a gas station. They're parked alongside each other, nose to tail, swatting criminals. "You gotta watch out for cops, too. That's another thing."

I park in the lot next to an Italian sports car. As we walk inside the building, we can feel the air conditioning gone haywire. It's still too early for refrigeration, and the office feels like an ice box, the kind Roy and my dad used to have to stock—with ice—when they were kids. Allyson smiles and says, "Hello, Mr. Conway!"

"Howdy."

"Howdy," she says, smiling. "Howdy!"

I take Roy down the hall and introduce him to Goldstein. "Chuck," I say, "this is my uncle, Roy Conway."

Goldstein stands, coming around from his desk; he offers his hand and says, broadly, "Pleased to meet you, Roy."

And the odd thing is, Roy believes it. You can tell by the way he looks around the room at all the diplomas and degrees, the paper on the wall, that he actually believes it.

Back at the reception desk, Allyson's looking at the switchboard, the lights and all the people in the offices talking. When I reach for a pen, she puts her hand on mine and says, "He's cute. He's really, really cute."

Now she's leaning, forward, so I can see what she knows I know is still available.

"So," she says, still leaning. "How's Kathleen?"

The smart thing to say would be something like *I don't date women at work,* but since this is my first real job, and since

I only work part-time, it's not likely to carry much weight. Also it might turn out to be a lie, same as saying *I'm going to get married.* I know enough about legal conventions to know I don't believe in them. Kathleen called last night. She lives in Philadelphia now, and she called me up at three A.M. to let me know she still wants to call me up. When she asked if I'm still living with my cousin, I said, "It's not something you really want to know."

"I know. I know. But still you could think about me."

"You're right. I could."

Paul Newman would have never said this, but then his script never called for this situation. Instead he would have asked Kathleen if she needed money, or if she was being treated badly by someone he used to go to school with. I don't think I went to school with anyone Kathleen knows, or sleeps with, and even if I did what good would it do to say anything? We're talking a lot of water under the bridge by now.

In Tempe, Arizona, the Salt River is dry nine months out of the year. Even so, when the rains do come, people always worry about the bridges flooding out, teenagers in four-by-fours get drowned, it's a dangerous time of year. Roy, he understands this kind of thing, and on the way back, we stop at a strip-joint not far from home. The River Bottom.

Inside the room is full of smoke and perfume and lonely men. Roy and I take a table ringside, we order a couple beers, and then a couple shots, and after a couple more Roy is feeling fine. He's explaining *testators* to me. He keeps an eye on the girls.

Roy takes a swig. "You're never too old," he says, coughing, waving his hand. "Know what we used to call this kind of place? Back in my day?"

"What's that?"

"A first-class joint. That's what! That's what we called it!"

I get up and go to the phone and try Kathleen. Her phone is out, imagine that, and suddenly I have this vision:

Annie—standing up there on stage, straddling a beam. I see her wrapping her fine legs around a beam, tossing her hair, and I'm thinking this is what happens. This is what happens to girls who don't know better, or girls who know us better than we think we do. Tanga, the girl in leopard skin, she can't be more than twenty. She's younger than me and trying to dance the way they do on TV, as if this were *Star Search* and one of us just might really be an agent. The manager, a fat guy with a .38, says they come in here all the time, *incognito*. I'm thinking this is the kind of thing Kathleen could never understand, and then across the bar, behind my Uncle Roy and ordering a beer, I see none other than J. Adams Powell. He's tipping the waitress and when he sees me, he holds up his glass and nods, slowly, as if we really have known each other for a long time.

You're not supposed to fall in love with your cousin. It's a basic rule that I'm still not quite aware of, and by that I mean I haven't yet decided I'm in love with Annie. As I see it, we're still just family. Love, like heredity, starts in the blood; it takes a while to bring things to a boil, even in Arizona. It's not as if I'm prepared to raise a family.

When I get Roy back to the farm, Annie helps me pour him into bed. He's floating on his bed and we're tugging at his boots. On the dresser is a picture of Roy with my dad: they're both in their twenties, they have their arms wrapped around each other, they're wearing hats. Only the quality of the photograph lets you know how long ago this was. I pull off Roy's pants and take out his wallet. I remove two twenties.

Annie looks at me, and I say, "I need to borrow the truck."

"Okay."

I walk down the hall, slowly, measuring my stride, and Annie follows behind. She rests her hands on my shoulders, and when we reach the kitchen, she turns me to face her. She places my callused hand on her heart.

"I'm not adopted," she says, kissing me. "Drive safe."

The truck's a '64 Chevy with a three-speed column. Under the seat Roy keeps a bottle of Beam, and as I make my way through Buckeye, I stop to use the phone, and Kathleen's doesn't answer for the very last time. I gas up both tanks and pick up a six to keep me going. It's a long drive, six hours over the top of I-10, and I think there are other things I could be doing right now. I could be going over my notes. I could be watching TV with Annie, our feet on the coffee table, maybe accidentally touching. I'm thinking all this is something I want to understand, and I'm telling myself I want to do the right thing. Meanwhile, I cruise behind a semi doing seventy plus. I remind myself I'm breaking the law and toss my empties on the floor. I keep a look out for speed traps and, finally, when I begin my descent into the territory of LA, I turn on the radio and listen to the weather.

J. Adams came through all right. Once in court, Goldstein called Mrs. Gertrude Simms to the stand. He asked her, politely, which testicle it was she had allegedly seen. When she couldn't answer, Goldstein brought out a spread from *Playgirl*. Pointing, he asked her, "Was it this one? Or did it look more like this?"

"I don't know."

"This one, the one on the right?"

"I don't know."

"That would be your left, of course."

It's all in the transcripts. J. Adams paid six and a half grand to have his record cleared, and three months later he married the daughter of a state senator. Now he owns a car dealership and rumor has it he's thinking about running for governor. Meanwhile, he sells Japanese imports on Indian School, and you can see him late at night, on the TV, explaining low financing.

When I took Annie out to dinner, at Rick's, she wore her best dress—white, cotton, from a designer shop in a mall—and ordered wine bravely. White wine, while I had a Bud, and she told me stories about her mother, a steak house waitress in Denver. Apparently, her mother mistook Roy for an oil baron, the kind from Dallas before the glut, and most men or boys Annie dated didn't seem to be much different from Roy.

"I could go to college," she said. "I just don't know why. I remember you, though. In Montana. You showed me a creek and called it Conway Creek, like you named it. College can't teach you what you don't already want to know."

And what I thought about, driving, was what I wanted Kathleen to know.

The driveway was full—Kathleen's and some foreign car, so I parked on the lawn, the headlights shooting into the living room of her apartment where she slept on a futon. I left the truck running, grabbed a beer and got out fast. I tried the door, locked, and did what any decent near-drunk man would do: kicked it in. By the third try I was inside amid candlelight and smooth jazz, Kathleen twisting in a sheet, her Berkeley-Boston boy looking for his glasses, tugging on his shorts. The telephone cord was unplugged and by it, on the floor, lay a pocket mirror smeared with coke.

"How's it going?" I said, tossing him the beer.

"It's not how it looks," he said, shaking. He reached toward Kathleen, giving her the beer, and I watched her face looking at the beer and what all this was going to mean. She still didn't get it.

"So what are you going to say," I said. "I'm sorry? I mean is that what you really want to say?"

"I'm sorry," said the guy. "Really. Hey, I'm really, really sorry."

And then it clicked: Kathleen took the beer and threw it at me, a good solid throw that caught me in the chin. I stood there rubbing at my chin, taking her in one last time while she let go of the sheet. She let it fall and smiled up at me.

"It's warm," she said, pointing. "The beer, I mean."

And then I left. I left leaving the door open the way I

wanted her to remember it: swinging on its hinges because nothing is simply open and shut.

There's not a man alive who doesn't have to be afraid of those things he's still capable of doing. I stopped at a diner, ordered two cups of coffee to go, and drove off—heading east, into the sunrise, which seemed to be a pretty fine closing argument.

Most things are relative. I walked by Goldstein's office one night and stopped to listen to Allyson, spread-eagled on his desk, knocking the pictures of Goldstein's children across the room. It would be nice to say Goldstein left his wife for her, but he didn't. He didn't even have a wife, just a lot of kids and alimony. Later Allyson took a job at a dentist's office across town where she increased her take-home pay twelve percent. As for the farm, it's long been turned into condos.

But two weeks later, I'm moving hay in the south paddock—five hundred bales worth. I'm bucking bales and Annie rides up, bareback, on top of Donovan. She's been working him regularly; he's beginning to develop some manners. Overall, he really is a fine horse, and when she rides up, she tells me Roy wants to see me. Something about property values and tax shelters, the kind of thing he needs to talk to me about. Often when Annie kisses me, she kisses me on the mouth, and we both know by now what's going to happen to us. We both know I'm going to want to kiss her back, and so, standing there, admiring the fine light of day, I grab my shirt and swing on up behind her. I swing up on Donovan's spine and Annie takes my hands. She takes my hands around her waist. I can feel the sweat soaking through her t-shirt, and what I'm thinking, simply, is that this is everything I know. I'm thinking there's only what you do in life, and then what happens next. I'm thinking of this girl, and the back of her neck, and the way my body fits around her.

"Hold tight," she says, lifting the reins. "No. Tight."

All We Shall

As for Kentucky, she writes, *I've heard some lovely things. I've heard they've got the Irish down there, hidden away like berries, eager to be sweet.*

She writes at a small, round table in her living room where the light is strong. Outside the pines sway heavily in the wind. On her front lawn sits the painter's truck, a white truck covered with paint spills, and she thinks it odd that painters always wear white, and never gray, or blue. Against the green grass the white seems bright to her even now. She listens, too, for the sounds of paint being scraped away from the walls of her house, the steady knocking at the wood. Her landlord, a retired police officer, has decided to have the house painted—summer work, summer chores. Yesterday, after returning from her trip to the coast, Maine, six days of driving across the span of the country, she found the northern face of the house sticky with paint. To the south the wall was still dirty and gray, shedding its skin, and it made her feel sad, the difference—a sudden rush of sadness.

Change, she writes, *alters my vision of things. Classes start next week, and I'm anxious, unsettled. It feels odd to be back.*

She is writing to Conor, almost old enough to be her brother, Ian, who has recently died. Conor is her student, the one with whom she had an affair, last semester, during the spring while the snow began to melt. A night class, so that at night, with the thin pages of their texts turning through the pages of British poetry and prose, into the increasingly warmer months, March, and then April, the snow had seemed to recede by itself with nobody watching. Each morning they woke, a little more would be gone.

And before each class, the light seemed to linger, stretching out the days, making each one just a little bit more long. The class would meet once a week to discuss the major works; most needed to fill an elective, and this was available: *McCARTHY: BRIT LIT II TH: 7–9:30.* Some were expecting a man, probably a beard, maybe a little tweed. Instead she had given them tits and ass and long, red hair which came from her mother's side. She wore lingerie beneath her skirts and sweaters. She carried a portfolio full of their weekly papers, their brief, sometimes honest, always stilted efforts toward understanding. When asked by a thin, balding woman who sat in the third row if she were married, she had replied, "Sometimes." And then she had looked to Conor, in the back, leaning, his legs propped against a chair, and turned crimson.

It was a question, like the one about her age, she would often leave unanswered. A spiritual marriage, she thinks— wedded to the extreme: reason and lust, heaven and hell, sister and brother. Among her lovers, she preferred the androgynous.

"Colleen," Conor would say, his hand in her hair. "I love calling you Colleen."

This morning, when she woke, pulled from her Halcion and sleep, she was greeted by the painter, outside her open window, scraping away. She sat up clutching her sheet and asked what time it was, then lay back down to watch the light. She was afraid to rise fully, to begin the processes of her day: water for the coffee; food for her English setter, William Butler, whom she simply calls Billy; the wide, empty desk, waiting for her to start a chapter, this one on

Blake, the one she should have finished in May before she left for her parents' and somewhere, along the way, cracked up. Instead she returned briefly to her bed, to the calm quiet of her pillows where nothing but the patterns of sleep might take hold: the quiet of premeditated, undisturbed quiet, until the rhythm of the scraping began to alarm, the rattle of the shifting scaffolds, the vision of this man dressed in white scraping at the sides of her house. She rose quickly, found her robe where she must have left it, on the floor beneath the foot of her bed, and gave the man a show. He was a polite man, she realized, because he turned away, the scraping stopped, the moment he noticed.

"Thank you," she said. She turned to face the window, partially dressed, and said, "Would you like some coffee?"

She took Billy for a run, a hard run, seven miles to sweat out the sleep. She ran hard down San Francisco, across Santa Fe, into the campus and on through the mall with Billy at her side, loping along, panting and happy. In Maine, along the coast, Billy had run in the ocean, his paws steeped in the tide. There she had watched from the rocks, had sat with her father, finally talking. Ian, who had moved home during the last months, until his blood count forced him back to the hospital, in Portland, and then Indianapolis, of all places— Ian was dead now. Eight months worth at twenty-four from testicular cancer. "Cancer for the nuts," he called it. The cancer had spread up and into his throat like ivy. The house was covered with ivy, across the long, open porch, where her mother sat, watching the water and rocks, the remains of her family.

Colleen sat with her father on a rock, watching the water, and her dog splashing at its borders. "It was good to visit," Colleen said.

"Can't you find a job a little closer?"

"It's over," she said, thinking it was. "I'm better."

"Ghosts," he said, seriously. "You mustn't worry about

ghosts. If they're going to bother you, they will. Ian, he's a good ghost. I remember him with his hair."

Ian's hair, red, like their mother's, had fallen in sheets. It had fallen away with the weight of his muscle until he became bones, covered with skin—opalescent, opaque. When she left in November, during Thanksgiving break, she had kissed him good-bye, gently, on the head—the smooth tender dome of his skull. And then he had said, "Find yourself a man, Colleen. The kind you want to be with," and that's when she knew he thought he was going to die.

"I like you this way," she said. "You're growing generous."

"I can't think," he said, pointing to the door. "I can't talk. I can't."

And later, during Christmas, after he vomited Hi-C and stomach acid, she would bathe him and make him rinse his mouth. She would bathe him with a sponge and talk to his blood cells, nonsense whispers, talk talk talk about one being connected to another and another, like words in a sentence, or poem, and Ian would smile, nodding with the rhythm until he began to drift. At night, when he couldn't sleep, she would come into his room and there they would tell all the jokes they could remember until each was no longer funny. Sometimes she would run a bath and watch him while he soaked, in the water with candles to hide the scars, and there wouldn't be any talking now, just the water and light, and the understanding that he knew he was going to die and that somehow, for some reason, it just wasn't good enough. And she would think of their Granny's, in Clonmel, where they had spent their summers—across the ocean far, far away. As far away, it seemed, as Flagstaff, Arizona.

If you put an Irishman in bed with a naked woman, what does he reach for first? A beer.

It began St. Patrick's Day: slowly, at first, in her office, nipping at a bottle of Jameson's, just for the occasion, grading papers, nipping, sitting back to stew, her feet on the desk, the outside growing dusk in the cool parade of March—all those people passing by her office window in jackets and boots, and the ROTC boys, bellowing by . . . *She won't do it but her sister will!* She could feel the cold from her window, which was closed, seeping into her office, and the fresh, wildly surreal edge of danger this night seemed always to evoke: if you wanted it bad enough, anything could happen. Tonight, a night when people foreign unto themselves embraced because they wanted to, as if prodded into desire by St. Patrick himself—the celibate straining for relief. Like the dogs, or a naked man standing in a field alone, the moon seemed to howl, and she knew now where this was headed, and she knew it was the whiskey. That sweet, Irish whiskey. The whiskey had made her wet, and she felt it, slowly, in her office with the growing dusk. She felt it spread inside her like a dream.

Wine, Yeats wrote, comes in at the mouth. *And love comes in at the eye.* At the bar, Spanky's, she recognized her students, her colleagues, the new director of rhetoric and composition, Demain, who couldn't wait to bed her down. She giggled at the thought, imagined him beneath her, designing a rubric by which to measure his efficiency, her pleasure, that which she had learned thus far in the mountains. "But it's lonely in the mountains," he might say, and she giggled further, nursing a green beer, telling herself to go slow. There's always time. And slowly she watched the people, the people in green clothes and hats, the students with their legs in their jeans, wonderful legs, and hair—all these beautiful people. She was speaking with Joel, from the history department, and Misty, his narcoleptic wife, and someone from philosophy; she was describing her house, the fading paint, even, and how it looked in the snow. The little gray house on the white snow. She was nursing her beer, telling herself, slow, slow, and caught Conor's eye, which caught hers. And later, she'd catch it again, from across the bar, and still later, when he came sauntering up, easily, mug in hand, wearing fatigues and a sweater and his long, decidedly long hair, to where she stood listening for the rhythm of his voice: Kentucky. And then when he finally said, "Hey, Dr. McCarthy," his voice like fine, lovely wine, she realized Conor was drunk. So beautiful and drunk.

Once outside, on a long, quiet street, she watched herself stumbling into him, dizzy with grief.

I look at you, and I sigh . . .

She reaches for her tea. Billy lies in his corner, thumping his tail, and she waits for the balance, the equipoise. The painter is still outside, sitting now on the open tailgate of his truck, eating a sandwich. He eats slowly and studies the walls of the house, his measured progress, and she thinks he must be a kind man—the way he eats his sandwich, the way he looks away when he sees her looking. He seems embarrassed for having wakened her.

If it had been any different, Conor, would we still be the same?

The problem is how to breach the distance. Ethics aside, the space between them has been unbearably brief, a space trespassed upon by the very breadth of their skin, their seemingly endless supply of tangled flesh. Coming, she would see Ian, the white of his skin depleted of cells, blanched and ethereal. Her sheets were the color of hay, the color of early morning light, when the sun is still a dim and slowly rising figure. She would watch the light rise over his body, the curve of his shoulder, his hip, rising up and over the sill into her room becoming the light of day. On the morning after, in March, in the clear light of reason, she had risen first to shower: cold water, the color of ice, and when she returned to her room, shaken, still naked and weak, she had pulled the covers from her bed and watched him sleep. Eventually he woke, and just as he began to say her name, *Colleen,* she drew his finger to her lips. There, she felt it flutter, as if against her ribs.

I was raised a Catholic girl, blessed with purity and light. And you . . . And you? You, I think, were merely blessed.

Ian died in Indianapolis on the fourteenth of January: his family in attendance, in the hospital, wearing white surgical masks and rubber gloves. Once removed, the gloves left a faint powder on your skin, and you could smell the rubber, still on your fingers, hours later like condoms. The funeral and wake followed on the eighteenth, near their home, and after, on the twenty-first, classes for the Spring semester began. The timing considerate, Colleen said good-bye and caught a flight.

Where Ian had been before, Clonmel, he had gone to clear his head—at their Granny's, herself now gone, haunting her own house where Ian had lived alone reading his books. He had left the States, had washed out of law school, had gone to rinse himself clean of torts and briefs and rules. "If I'd stayed," he told Colleen. "If I'd stayed, the sins of the flesh . . . they linger." He still had his hair then, and she knew he couldn't stay, either. She knew that he belonged far away. They should be distant, separate. And later they had needed illness to fill in that distance—something inexplicable and random. A swollen testicle. Something people could believe in and feel sad about.

Outside, the painter stops. He pokes his head in through the living room window and says, "Excuse me, Miss?"

Startled, she tries to remain polite.

"Can I use your restroom?"

"Of course," she says, straining, uncomfortable, but knowing at the same time it's not exactly his fault. She expects him just to step on in through her open window.

Instead he climbs down the ladder and walks around the house to the front door, where Billy waits to receive him, like any other ordinary house guest.

"It's okay," he says at the door, apparently rushed. "I'll find my own way."

And now he is brushing past her, down the hall, and to the left.

After her run she took a bath. Conscious of the painter's presence, she drew the blinds. She drew the blinds and ran a bath, deep enough to soak, reading through the stacks of her mail. She saved for last a letter from Conor, now at home and looking for work. A boy with a degree. He told her about the chiggers and heat, the hot wet heat that made you sweat, always, persistently, which was so unlike the desert mountain air. He told her finally in the closing paragraph all about his *soul,* the way he felt it growing now, *like violets,* and how *you never know what you're going to love until you have to.* He wrote elliptically, as if precision might be too much, the way after the need was over even the slightest touch would make you flinch, scream, even—*thin skin,* he wrote. *I love your thin skin, Colleen,* and he was right, it was excessive, more than she wanted, and she found herself alone, in this tub with the painter somewhere outside and her dog, Billy, lying on the rug watching her read. The letter grew wet, pages and pages of ink, until some of the ink began to bleed and she felt as if she might really scream, just might really let go and do it until she realized she couldn't remember the last time she had screamed, that the last time was something she had been told about—a foggy, oddly curious anecdote. In Maine, she was told, near the water and rocks where she had screamed at the sky, during a storm, one night after dinner: pot roast, potatoes, wine. And now if she did scream the painter would be sure to intrude, and she was beyond that now. She was beyond everything but herself. So she pulled herself under and listened for the water, the pages in her hands: clutched above her waist and dripping into the tub.

The letter was old, two months, and she knew he would be waiting. He would be watching his mailbox, every day, hoping for something to drop inside. Something with his name on it. Anything with his name and the handwriting she had used to correct his papers, over and over again. In her office, he would be shy, sullen. He would say, "Yeah, but, what the hell?" and she would say back, testing, "Yeah, what the hell? This really sucks," and he would lighten up, eager to receive—advice, hope, promises. His presence, disquieting as it was, gave her something to watch for during the long silent times between her classes: an unexpected encounter on the lawn, at the cafe—a hopeful look over a double cappuccino. "Dr. McCarthy," he might say, "all I want to do is pass!" and she would say, just as rehearsed, "All we ever do is pass. We have to try harder."

Meanwhile, Demain, of Denver, is sniffing at her skirt, however metaphorically: inviting her out, stopping by to chat, searching, always, for a glimpse down her blouse—a patch of pale, sullen flesh. At times she thought it sad, this man of the praxis with no one to listen, let alone feel; a man in need of encounter, regardless. Other times, she thought him hopelessly comical, a man whose sole purpose in life was words, the encouraging of bad discourse, as if words and one's ability to abuse them might in fact be enough. Which it wasn't, ever. Words, even those well-placed, were merely things to take you places—like sex, a mode of transport. All great writing is sex, and all great sex is touch, and where it pushed you to. What you wanted was *idea*—the inexpressible core you felt in the bones of your feet. The knot in your belly, the heart in your throat. What you wanted was Conor walking down the mall with his jeans torn at the knees, a long trench coat and his life packed in a bookbag, smiling and saying, "McCarthy, we gotta do a beer! We just gotta!"

How was I to know? she writes. *How were you to know? How were we to know already that sweet taste of ourselves?*

Conor, Conor, Conor . . . say it long enough, and you grow convincing.

When I was little I was a girl; I was young and little and still knew more about others than myself. So too with Ian, a boy, my brother. Together we looked alike. We looked alike, Conor: skin, eyes, hair, the same freckles. We'd swim in the ocean or play IRA and were it not for our genitalia, who's to say who we were? Who's to say, Boy, over there, and, Girl, there. See? See them both? Can you even see them underneath the sun? Underneath the moon?

Can you even see them?

Desire, she thinks, is a mode of transport. And she will tell him he took her places lovely and beyond reach. But she is back now, she writes. *I'm back.*

Where she went in Maine she's still uncertain. It was a land of heavy medication, clean linens and long, quiet walks. After her release, her mother would bring her tea, toast, would ask her if she'd like her to sit. "It's been just too much," her mother would say, and Colleen would nod, holding her words, still unwilling to give them up. She held onto her words for six weeks, writing only the briefest of messages, and when she finally did let go, when she finally did let go at the sky, after dinner, standing on the rocks outside dressed only in her robe, she prayed to God for lightning. She prayed to God for a swift, catholic and apostolic glimpse of eternity—here, in her breast, which she bared even for God: a steady, throbbing target. Here where she wanted to be struck, like Leda, taken into a white rush. She wanted to come to God on a swift rod of righteousness and lay herself clean, there upon a table of blessedness and light, there upon a table where the sins of the flesh lay heaped damp as clover.

And while the storm was fierce, the waves high as herself, there was still no lightning. Only rain, inexhaustible, and cold.

When Ian came back, it killed him. She will have to be careful. She will have to labor slowly—to embrace the realm of *idea* when only it is safe. *Words,* she thinks. *I'll have to measure my words* . . . and what she remembers is that first class, back in January, searching the dark sky for something to say, and the cold, and Conor, timid and pale in the last row wearing a green sweatshirt, raising his hand, and the tremendous weight of all that responsibility. And she remembers telling herself, *I can do this. I really can.*

Outside, the painter is moving a ladder. It is a long, wooden ladder, and still his clothes are white. When he swings the ladder near the window she catches his eye, and he sees her, looking up from her table. He watches her wonder about the color of things. And he knows, too, that she knows what he's thinking. She knows that he is hungry. *You're painting my house,* she wants to tell him. *You're covering it up and I don't understand your clothes and you're still out there* and now he smiles, opening his hand, briefly, to wave. For a moment he loses his balance, and the ladder quivers, slightly, just overhead.

Where I've been, she will write, *is where I am.*

. . . *and what you must understand, Conor, is I loved my brother. I loved him the way a boy loves the moon, the way a girl drinks from the sea until she's bloody and full. And I wanted to. And I want you to find it. I want you to find a woman, the kind you need, the kind who'll rip your heart out and rub it slowly over the skin of your body.*

Over your knees, Conor. Over your bones.

The Dark Part

Most people wanted to talk about my mother, who had killed herself, and I had to sing this song. There was money involved. A thousand-dollar savings bond and a small part in the Flagstaff Summer Opera. At the time, Flagstaff was three hours north, in the mountains, and I'd never been there by myself.

It was the year I stopped going to confession and worked at Safeway bagging groceries. Usually I slept in my father's truck, an old Jeep with off-road lights and orange carpet squares in back. I kept my tools in a wooden chest I'd made in Shop—an ax, waterproof matches, jumper cables. I called it my Survival Chest and would think about the day the Communists invaded Los Angeles, and then Phoenix, and I'd be safe hiding out in the mountains. On the lid carved into the wood were my initials (*WM,* for Walker Miller), and after Karen Kalko discovered my initials were the same forwards (*WM*) and upside-down (*WM*) she convinced me to join Honor Choir. Karen had been my girlfriend for three weeks, and even if it wasn't quite right, she wanted us to have a lot in common.

"You should feel privileged," she said. "Most girls never make it. They *want* to be in Honor Choir."

We were sitting on the lawn in front of the gym. I was still sweating, because the rule saying we had to shower hadn't been made yet, and I had only played volleyball in Ms. Williams's class *Sports for Life.* Ms. Williams taught History and PE, and I liked to take her class. Also she looked a little like my mother, when my mother was still in college, with short hair and glasses.

And on the lawn Karen Kalko was sort of pretty—earrings and hair, pink button-down shirt, but she didn't look like anyone I really knew. I kept leafing through my Shop book, a chapter on cabinet making to remind myself of the parts I really understood, when Karen said, "Well anyway, try it."

She gave me a flier with pictures of the last seven Honor Choirs, most of which looked the same.

"Try it," she said, standing.

When I watched her walk away, I didn't worry about the way I smelled. Instead I looked at the flier and thought I'd never seen so many lonely-looking girls in all my life.

If I knew about girls now what I didn't know then, it probably wouldn't matter. Karen Kalko was going to go to the university in Flagstaff for either Pre-Law, Pre-Med, or Anthropology. I was supposed to work at Safeway and save money, while she made more plans, and then I got fired.

My father had been a captain in the Navy, and when you are seventeen, you are still young enough to have a best friend, though usually it's not your father. Mine was Howie Bently, who was on the wrestling team and broke a lot of rules and never, never had a girlfriend. The night after I was fired, the night before my big audition, Howie sprayed open a beer and became philosophical. We were in the back of my father's truck, under the carport with the radio blasting. It was the kind of thing that usually bothered the neighbors.

"Face it," Howie said. "You and your old lady might as well be married. You're whooped."

"I'm unemployed," I said.

"She's got you by the balls. Hard, fast, and doomed. And Newborn," he said, laughing, handing me a beer. "Newborn!"

Doomed was another Howie word, like *old lady,* and Mr. Newborn was nice enough, but he wasn't very healthy. He was tall and pale and seemed to attract flies. There we'd be, our mouths all agape, going *ooh* right on up the scales, or *Oklahoma!,* my favorite, and these flies would come in through the door and land on his head, or nose, even his ears. And then he'd try and brush them away, without messing up our instructions, but in general the Honor Choir never paid much attention to his instructions, anyway. After all, this wasn't the Navy, and Mr. Newborn would stop, laugh, shifting his feet, which were huge, and never get mad at the flies. When he'd tell us to stand up straight, he'd tell us to stand up straight like God's children—on the legs God gave us. Whenever he wanted to start talking, the piano player, Iva Polanski, would stop playing and we'd all stand still and polite until we got bored. Meanwhile, Karen stood behind me in the third row and, singing, I'd listen for her voice, but what I liked most about the singing was the way the piano always sounded so nice no matter what the Honor Choir ever did.

A grocery store in Arizona is always cold. Outside it can be a hundred and fifty-seven degrees, dogs are getting brain damage in cars, ice cream is safe for maybe three, six minutes, but inside it's always cold. For the three months I worked at Safeway, I wore the same green tie I had borrowed from my father's closet and practiced being punctual. I never did learn to make it look right. Mr. Dean, the Day Manager, said I was a doornail and never showed up on time.

He said that to me just before he fired me, too. He said, "Face it, Wally. You're a doornail." Basically, said Mr. Dean, I just didn't have what it took to be in the grocery supply industry. He was referring to all the grapefruit I had thrown at the customers. He was referring to the fact that he thought I was turning crazy, which I probably was, though of course

I didn't know that then. When you think you are going crazy, you basically feel the way you always do; you just start acting a little differently, like my mom, before she killed herself. Or like the Captain, sitting all alone in his car, reading old love letters all by himself.

"I know you've got family problems," Mr. Dean said, shaking my hand. "Good luck to you."

Iva Polanski didn't have a family. She was two years older than me and going to go to college in Berlin where she was born. She had short black hair, really short, like a flattop, and she lived with her aunt in Phoenix. She had skin like a baby. I mean like a cherub, or angel—that kind of skin. Next to all those lonely girls in Honor Choir with feathered hair and blue eye shadow, Iva Polanski was exotic.

In the afternoons she'd practice with me for my audition. She'd play out her part of "Oklahoma!"—the song that best showed off my range, Mr. Newborn had said—and I'd watch Iva's hands, standing behind her near the shaved parts of her neck; or beside her, and when she'd lean over the keys you could see down the hollow of her shirt. It wasn't a very steep hollow, just smooth brown skin. The skin poured over the big bone in the center of her chest. She wore t-shirts with her gypsy skirts, and sometimes, especially when it was hot, the t-shirts stayed close, and she'd play along, stop, look up at me and smile. She even had exotic teeth, straight and unevenly white. I can honestly say now that I have always been in love with Iva Polanski, even before I ever met her; it was that kind of feeling you just happen to know is real, and true, and maybe lonely, she was that beautiful. For example, sometimes, playing along on the piano, she'd stop and stretch. Once she said she missed her boyfriend, who climbed up mountains in Utah and Idaho, but God knew where he was. Mr. Newborn had told us a choir was a room full of happy angels, happy and singing to God, and sometimes I'd picture my mother up there, singing, but I knew if you believed in God, and you killed yourself, you didn't get to hang around Him. My mother, I guess, was like most people; she wanted to be popular and famous.

After practicing, I'd meet Karen in her pink shirt and hair, at the Burger King, and we'd eat fries, and then I'd drive her home, because she wanted me to be her boyfriend. Most nights, we'd talk on the phone. On Wednesdays, she had to be home by eleven o'clock; midnight on Fridays; Saturday was Family Night; and she had told me last week, on Tuesday, that she liked me an awful lot.

"I like you an awful lot, Walker," she had whispered on the phone. "I don't care what happened."

The phone was making my ear sweat, and I was thinking an awful lot about Iva, and later I realized it was kind of like being married. It was like being told to believe in something. It was like, as Howie had put it, being had by the balls.

Of course no one had ever touched my balls—especially Karen; it was just an expression, and I was beginning to get depressed. With Howie, sitting in back of my father's truck, under the carport and thinking too much. Karen was home watching HBO with her sisters. My father was out with the Recently Single Catholic Men's Club. Howie was on his fourth beer, and I decided that what I really wanted to do was practice Survival Driving Techniques.

"Look," Howie said. "It was just a job."

"Howie," I said, "let's practice."

We loaded up the beer and climbed up front. We drove out past Pima Road, mostly desert, with Howie throwing beer cans at the signs. After a while we headed east, toward some gullies in the direction of New York, another place I'd never been, and then we started doing doughnuts and figure-eights, flying all over the ruts and stirring up the landscape. The dirt was dry and the dust flew everywhere in the lights—bright yellow dust, just like day, and it was working fine, too, I was feeling better already, better than reading Shop, really, when the rear end slid hard into a saguaro.

A saguaro weighs about thirty thousand pounds. Everything stopped. Howie was in my lap, still holding his beer, and the dust was floating all around us in the light. Then there was this noise, this quiet noise while the engine ticked in the heat and the saguaro began to lean. You could hear it stretching and pulling at its roots, which according to Mr. Langousis are naturally shallow, as it leaned and broke in half right behind us.

"Wow," Howie said, finishing off his beer. "Look what you've gone and done now, Walker."

Tragedy is what happens when you don't think anything will. Usually it happens once during a lifetime, sometimes a lot more, and sometimes when it happens bad enough you know it's going to take you a while to get over it, no matter who's to blame. For example, it takes a cactus a hundred years to even grow a foot.

I was in the produce section, hosing down the lettuce and squash, when I heard my name over the Muzak.

"Walker," said Jane. "Walker to the front, please."

I went up front and found Jane, *hustling.* She was ringing up nine hundred dollars of groceries—pickles, yams, light bulbs; it's amazing the things people like to eat. Behind the nine-hundred-dollar customer stood Ms. Williams.

"Hi, Ms. Williams," I said. "What'cha doing?"

Ms. Williams smiled, her ice cream cradled in her arms, and said, "Hello, Howie."

"No," I said, pointing at my name tag. "I'm Walker." Actually, the name tag said *Wally,* because that's what Mr. Dean called me.

"You're going to lose your ice cream," I said. It was slipping between her elbow and six-pack of diet soda. She balanced herself and stood there patiently, looking over the impulse items, her arms turning pink from all the air conditioning. I finished bagging the nine hundred dollars worth of groceries—juice in the bottom, bread on the top, just so. Then I loaded up three carts and pushed them out of the way. The lady began to write a check and she couldn't find her Safeway card. She kept talking to Jane, and Jane kept making eyes at the lady's kids. Ms. Williams stood behind waiting and shivered.

"Howie," I said, waiting for something to happen. "He's my friend."

"Yes," said Ms. Williams, smiling.

I wondered if she'd seen me in Shop, if that's why she had me confused. I said, "I'm in your class. Sports for Life. I really like it."

The lady was gone now, her kids pulling her carts like mules, and I was bagging Ms. Williams's groceries. "Double Strength or Regular?" I asked, trying not to notice her tampons. They were the same kind still under the sink in my parents' bathroom.

"What?"

"Doesn't matter," I said. "We only use Double Strength. Even our Regular Strength is really Double."

I set the two bags in a cart and began to wheel toward the door. We went through the double automatic doors into the bright sun. Outside it was warming up for summer, people in sandals and shorts, and we passed by the lady with her carts and all her kids.

"Howie," Ms. Williams said, "he's the boy whose mother . . ."

She let it trail off, the way most people do when they say something like that.

"Oh my God," she said. "That's you, too?" She brought her hand up to her mouth, as if it belonged there; it was the first time I ever really looked at a woman's hand. Her hand was pretty and her arm was covered with bracelets from Mexico. She didn't have any freckles.

"Sometimes," she said, "I don't know. Sometimes I just don't know where I am."

I was about to say something, to make her feel better, when a car full of kids came slowly driving by. It was so slow I could watch everything going on, like on the TV, when things are going slow which means really the people doing things are going fast, which is the way real things go. Fast.

"Hey!" said the driver to Ms. Williams, a kid from Welding. "Nice tits!"

And then I said something I shouldn't have. I mean if the kid from Welding had kept driving, maybe it would have blown over, but he stopped. A blue station wagon with hubcaps. Probably his mother's.

"What you say, Miller?"

I took the cart and slammed it into his mother's car. It bounced off and I picked it up, over my head, this time slamming it on the roof. The cart bounced off, groceries everywhere, and I picked it up again and I kept throwing the cart, screaming, and the kid from Welding was trying to do something and Ms. Williams was trying to hold me, and for a while, just for a little while, I couldn't feel anything and everything was absolutely going to go my way.

I'm told I did other things. The dark part, I now know, is that place where you go when everything's too bright: it's the dangerous part that's yours and all your own, and you could tell when my mother had gone away to visit—her eyes, the way she scraped her nails on the wallpaper and stopped singing with the radio. She'd stop cooking and sleep for days in the same nightgown. At night the Captain would prowl around the house looking for a place to read. He said this had been going on for years.

Actually, I got the announcement in Shop. I was on the lathe, turning the beginnings of a lamp I was going to give my father, when I heard my name, *Walker Miller,* which was actually the name of my father, only I was the second. Everyone in Shop started clapping, because I wasn't crazy yet, and I left for the principal's office, thinking about the way that sounded—my name, coming over the loudspeaker.

Mrs. Knudson, the secretary, brushed a woodchip from my hair. She looked sad, as if she'd just realized she couldn't get new carpet, and then she led me into the principal's office. The office was full of green and blue furniture, and the principal, Mr. Buckner, seemed surprised to see me. On Tuesdays and Thursdays, Mr. Buckner wore aloha shirts to show he was normal.

"I'm Walker," I said. "Walker Miller."

He told me to sit down and asked Mrs. Knudson to leave the door ajar. He looked through a file. It had my name written in blue ink across the top; the ink was from a ballpoint pen and had smeared, and I knew that inside the file was a picture of me from junior high when I was still wearing braces. Then there was the time I snuck inside the girls' locker room. Mr. Buckner closed the file, checked his watch and said, "Walker, there's been an accident."

"What kind of accident?"

"It says here you're Catholic. Is that correct?"

"I guess."

"Would you like me to call a priest?"

"What kind of accident?"

And then he told me. My father's doctor had called from the hospital, where my father was now admitted *to rest.* Mr. Buckner left out the details—he didn't know them—but they were still there. The razors and blood, the Jacuzzi in my parents' bedroom. And my mother, under the skylight, a half-finished bottle of champagne and a piece of her stationery with nothing on it. The paper had fallen into the water and turned pink except for the embossed part with her initials.

Mr. Buckner came around his desk and took me by the

shoulder. I could see his shirt, all full of flowers tied up together, and then he said, "Honestly. Is there someone I can call?"

The story behind Ms. Williams was this: when she was in college, she posed almost completely nude for a magazine, something about Volleyball Girls and Southern California, and eventually I found out. Naturally, I promised myself in general to keep it secret. I kept the picture folded up safe in my wallet, and Iva said it made her really sad, the look on Ms. Williams's face, standing on a beach in California like that.

"Yeah," I said. "But she's really pretty, don't you think?"

"She's sad," Iva said. "That's why she's so pretty."

By now we were practicing every day at Iva's house. Her piano, a brown upright, stood in a corner of her bedroom, and we sat on the bench while we practiced. Her room was full of flowers and drapes and a picture of her boyfriend who climbed up mountains; he is standing in the middle of a canyon wearing sunglasses and jeans. Probably, he's twenty.

Iva caught me looking at her boyfriend, who didn't look sad at all.

"You know—" Iva said, turning to face me. She pulled her legs up and crossed them on the bench, smoothing her skirt and leaning. "You know, I'm not sure singing is really what's best. I mean, there's lots of other things you can do in college. You don't have to sing."

"I can't take Shop."

"Yeah," she said, nodding. "But it's not like you really have to sing, either." She smiled and pulled at her toes. She sat there pulling on her brown toes and shook her head. She took my hands, studying my fingers. She looked at my fingers and said, "You could play piano, Walker. If you wanted."

"No," I said. "I tried once."

"You know why you try something? You try it because

you think you can do it better than anybody else. You try it because you think you can sing or play piano or climb mountains better than anybody living. And you know the sad part? The sad part is you can't. You try real hard, but you just can't."

She gave me back my hands and kissed me, quickly, before we'd have time to think about it.

"And then what?" she said.

I mean Iva Polanski was mature, and beautiful; she dated a guy who climbed up mountains and lived on his own. And I know now that most things in life, especially the nice things, like Iva Polanski, are a gift. Like talent, and what you are supposed to do with it, even if you don't have much.

While my father was in the hospital, resting, I stayed at Howie's. Mrs. Bently was nice and asked me what I liked to eat. His dad who took a lot of medication let me park my father's truck in his backyard, though he only let me and Howie drive it to practice for our driver's license test: we practiced parallel parking between garbage cans. At night we slept in the same room with bunk beds, Howie on the bottom, me on the top, and when Father Lawson came to visit, I asked him to go away. Father Lawson had told me about the Church Softball Team for Teens, and when I asked him to go away, I asked politely. I didn't want to hurt his feelings.

Sometimes I'd still think about my mom. That night, the night of the great cactus tragedy, Howie and I sat in the back of the truck looking over the sky. The beer was turning warm, the radio played, we were growing more and more philosophical. All around us was desert and air, lit up like a football game, just for us.

"Really," Howie said. "What's the old lady like?"

He meant Karen Kalko, who had reversible initials, and was my girlfriend. "She's Catholic," I said.

"I knew it," he said, laughing. "I just knew it."

Later, while I was still thinking about what that meant, *Catholic,* I told Howie that sometimes I liked to pretend that I was the only one I knew who was still alive. I thought about the people singing on the radio, and the way sometimes songs seemed as if they were just for you and what you were thinking about, and then I decided maybe I'd someday be able to do that—to make millions of dollars, to wear earphones in an insulated recording studio, making records. I'd start out with opera, in Flagstaff, get some experience. According to Mr. Newborn, tenors were gold. Maybe I'd even change my name to Vic, though actually, I was just trying to keep from feeling I was doomed.

Howie said, "You know what, Walker?"

"What?"

"I really think we ought to join the Navy."

Sometimes I felt that way a lot. If I had been an adult, I probably would have fallen in love with Ms. Williams. My father had been in the Navy—Captain, a sub tender in the Atlantic—but Howie wanted to be a SEAL. Lots of demolitions and girl spies in swimsuits, and the auditions for the Flagstaff Summer Opera were held at St. Peter's High in downtown Phoenix. Normally I worked Sundays, and I woke up unemployed feeling dizzy—my first hangover. At first I didn't know what to wear.

I picked up Iva at her aunt's. She was wearing a purple skirt and black tank top and she had only one earring on. From her doorstep, you could see the dent in the truck from the night before, the cactus we'd made tragic, and you could see some of the places where the primer showed through.

"You look nice, Walker," Iva said, pointing at my Safeway tie. I opened the door for her, to show I was mature, and we drove to St. Peter's, which was surrounded by chain-link fence; the parking lot was full of station wagons and signs that said, *No Smoking, Loitering, or Misbehavior.* After we found the right building, we sat in a hallway and said mean things about Mr. Newborn. The hallway smelled like old sneakers and vinegar, and when the door finally opened for my turn, a lady stepped out with a clipboard. From behind her rushed a girl, crying, her makeup smeared all over her face.

"Miller?" said the lady. "Walker Miller?"

Iva and I stood and walked into a room for gymnastics. A piano had been rolled in by the parallel bars, and there was white dust everywhere. A man with reading glasses sat in a wooden chair resting a tape recorder on his lap. I was the only one in the room wearing a tie. The woman smiled and asked who my companion was.

"Iva," Iva said.

The man smiled and said, "Hello, Iva."

"Hello," Iva said. She sat at the piano bench, tucking herself in.

"And what are you two going to perform for us today?" asked the man with the tape recorder.

"Oklahoma!" I said. "By Rodgers and Hammerstein."

The man nodded, taking notes, and said, almost smiling, "You may begin anytime, Mr. Walker."

"Miller," I said, wanting everything right. "Walker Miller."

"Yes, Mr. Miller. Anytime."

At first I was afraid I'd offended him, and then I thought, this guy doesn't know who the hell I am. Iva started playing, giving me the cue just like we'd planned. She started playing and I went into the song, trying hard to use my diaphragm, concentrating, remembering to use my hands and smile. It was a big gymnasium, even for gymnastics, and I was just going into the third page when I heard the sound of the tape recorder being shut off. I looked up and saw the man, then the woman, and stood still.

"Thank you, Wally," said the woman, loudly.

"Thank you, Iva," said the man. "That was very nice."

"We're all done," I said, looking at Iva. She gathered her

music and looked back at me, really nicely, and I knew I should be feeling nervous, or embarrassed, or sad. But instead I felt only this feeling that something long and not very important was finally over with—like Christmas, if you've ever had to spend it by yourself. You just want to get it over with.

That night, that night I was starting to feel doomed all over again, after all, I dropped Howie off at his house. All the lights were out; like normal people, his parents had been asleep for hours. He stood there in the street, the door open and leaning on the edge, making it sway, and said, "It's not just a job. It's an adventure!"

"Night, Howie."

"Maybe she thought it'd be better," Howie said. "You know, somewhere else. Maybe she thought it'd be better somewhere else. Like Indiana."

I'd never been to Indiana, either. Just Europe and the Mediterranean. Before he retired, my father had been stationed in lots of interesting places. I drove home thinking about Indiana, and other interesting places, and saw my father's car in the carport. He was inside his car with the light on, the radio blasting trumpet music. He was reading a letter.

"Hi," I said, coming around from behind the truck.

"Hi," he said. He turned down the radio, folded up the letter. Beside him on the car seat was a pile of letters and a loose, red hockey lace. In college my father had played hockey. He kept his skates in the bottom drawer of the desk in his den with my mother's letters. I'd read all of them long before she ever killed herself.

"Been drinking?"

"Just a couple. Over at Howie's. We drove into a cactus."

He shrugged and said, "I've been reading." He lit a cigarette and looked at the letters. "It's amazing, things she used to say. Your mother. You know she wanted to be like Joni Mitchell? She loved that kind of stuff. Just like you."

"I have a big day tomorrow. My opera audition."

"Father Jim asked about you. He says whenever you're ready, to give him a call. He says Dr. Ryan understands this kind of thing better than us. Dr. Ryan deals with it every day. It's his job and doesn't mean you're crazy."

"Okay."

"How's Karen?"

"Fine."

"That's good. She's a nice girl. A looker, you know? Karen. She's the marrying kind, that girl. She's the kind of girl you bring home to meet the Admiral."

"Okay."

And then my father started laughing. He hit his hands on top of the steering wheel and started laughing really hard. It was loud and filled the carport. He kept laughing and then he stopped and wiped his eyes. He reached through the car window and punched me softly in the arm.

Later, after I was put into the psycho ward, Dr. Ryan asked me lots of questions. He asked me, for example, "So why do you think your mother killed herself?"

At first I used to think maybe it was because of me. Then I thought it wasn't because of me, which made more sense, but was really a whole lot worse, and then one night I realized my father thought the same things—the strange parts in a song, the ones you keep coming back to over and over again because you've been taught to know them so well. I realized things weren't going to be all right, after all, and that probably, even if I had made the opera, I'd still have to explain things to people I'd never known. It made me feel better, kind of, knowing I was going to go talk to people who'd never even heard my name. It meant I could tell them anything. It meant I could change my name and start all over again and nobody, nobody would have to know I'd freaked out in the grocery store and decided to try and join the opera. Maybe I could still really be a rock star. I could really grow my hair long and learn to play guitar.

But after the audition, Iva and I went to her house. My head was feeling empty and I was trying hard not to think too much. We sat outside under the porch drinking lemonade with honey. Iva said it was good for a hangover; even drinking lemonade, she was mature and beautiful. "It replenishes the fluids," she said, and we sat beneath the porch, watching the sky, and always before, always before I'd thought when the time came, I'd know it. It would be something clearly understood and instinctual. For example, every time I looked at Karen Kalko, I knew she saw my mother, and every time I saw my mother, I saw someone who looked like a woman, but still it wasn't Karen. Instead I saw something dark and probably unexpected, and now here was Iva, breathing, truly alive, complicated as Biology.

When I followed Iva into the kitchen, she turned to me. She set down the pitcher of lemonade and put her hands on my waist. Behind her was a note tacked up on the fridge, a reminder to feed the pets, and she took my hand and placed it on her breast. And I remember thinking. I remember thinking this had never happened to me before.

"What?" she said, reaching for my tie.

I could feel a pulse, and I wasn't sure if it was hers or mine. But I wanted her to tell me. I mean I wanted her to be convincing.

Catholic, I think. I wanted her to say, *I'm Catholic.* I wanted her to say, *This is my body, which I give to you.*

Quick

If you looked, up through the dusk to the ledge of a small hill, you would see two boys. The boys are late for supper and collecting golf balls. Howie, the youngest, will turn eleven tomorrow night. "At midnight," he says. "October fifteenth."

Lucas points at a muddy ball half buried in the grass. "That's a dud," Lucas, who is sixteen, says. "It's old."

Howie reaches for it, anyway, and drops it into his suitcase. His suitcase is chartreuse, which means it once belonged to their mother. Because Lucas has a bone disease, he is not allowed to carry heavy objects. He wears a mask with an elastic band to keep germs from going in his mouth. Also, he is not allowed to drink from anybody's glass. Tonight they will have supper in the hotel restaurant, and Howie will order Chicken Teriyaki with Pineapple Sauce and a Chocolate Milkshake. As long as he finishes his plate, he is allowed to order milkshakes. Last night, he had Strawberry, and Lucas couldn't finish his Taco Salad.

Mr. Bently works for the government. Because of the hospitals in Phoenix, the *family* decided he should take a new post. Here he is going to monitor a corporation which fills a number of almost top secret defense contracts. Since Reagan became president, just a couple years ago, the corporation has stopped laying people off, which means *firing*. Mr. Bently was in the Army and went to Korea, where he learned to fire howitzers. "What's good for the government," Mr. Bently says, usually at dinner, "is good for us."

Now, because of the hot weather, he can wear his ties and white shirts with *short* sleeves. Mrs. Bently says their father is conservative, meaning the way he dresses. Since Lucas became sick, Mrs. Bently says grace before they eat, even in restaurants, and soon they will be permitted to move into their new house. They were supposed to move in yesterday, but the moving van broke down in Oklahoma. Inside the moving van are Howie's new hockey uniform and sled, and Lucas's *Encyclopedia of America,* and all their parents' furniture.

But now the two boys are standing on the ledge of a small hill where it is still possible to see them both. The sun is setting all around them, and Lucas says, looking at the chartreuse suitcase, which once belonged to their mother, "How many we got?"

"'Bout a thousand."

"We haven't got a thousand."

"Well, we've got a lot. Here," Howie says, handing Lucas the suitcase. "Feel."

2.

Neither knows very much about the sport of golf. While their parents have been kept busy settling matters for their new home, the boys have started lessons. Chip, who is tan and used to be a pro, likes to drink beer. He takes the boys to the practice range for thirty dollars an hour and says, "Golf is hard. Keep your eye on the ball."

Then he says, "Good swing."

They are staying at Golden Hills Country Club, because the hills are all golden. Actually, says Chip, the grass is badly watered, but in the distance you can see the Superstition Mountains. Even if it doesn't go anywhere, Howie likes to hit the ball, but Lucas is very serious. He wants to get the basics just right. Then, he says, he will move on to putting. Already Lucas has asked for his own set of clubs. Now Lucas wiggles his fingers and adjusts his grip, shifts his shoulders, greets the ball. He stops and turns to yell at Howie.

"Stop watching!" Lucas yells.

"I'm learning," Howie says. "Right, Chip?"

"Keep your eye on the ball," Chip says.

"I can't concentrate," Lucas says.

"You have to keep your eye on the ball," Howie says.

Lucas can't swing very hard, but still he makes the ball sail.

Chip gives off a low whistle. "You hooked that one, Luke."

"Lucas," Lucas says. "Is that good?"

"I want to play hockey," Howie says. "I hate golf."

"You slice some and you hook some," Chip says, sadly. "You learn to compensate."

And then Lucas falls down. He falls down on the yellow grass and doesn't let go of his club. He is lying on the grass, breathing hard; he tears off his mask and wipes his eyes. Finally, he sits up, his thin arms shaking, because of the disease inside his body. He sits up and says to Howie, "Well, did you hit anything?"

Now Howie lifts up his club, like a hockey stick, and takes a shot. Then he takes another. Now he is swinging at the dirt. He is swinging at the dirt over and over until his rented club breaks right in half.

3.

One night, now that he is eleven, Howie overhears his parents' conversation. His parents are sitting up late at the round table in the kitchen where Mrs. Bently keeps her books on and all the bills. The kitchen is also full of boxes waiting to be unpacked. Howie hears his parents say the words *bone* and *marrow* and *transplant.*

Later, alone in bed, he understands precisely what they mean. Lucas needs a *narrow bone.* One to replace the one that has gone bad and made him sick. Usually, Lucas is in the hospital bed, where the nurses talk to him a lot and give him apple juice. When you visit, you have to wear plastic gloves, and you aren't allowed to have a cold or a baby. In the hospital, Lucas's new golf clubs are standing by his nightstand, along with cards from all his classmates back in Wisconsin. When Howie goes to school, he walks all by himself. Always before he got to ride a bus. Now he walks to school and has a green bookbag his mother gave him for his birthday; blue is his favorite color, but they were out. His mother also gave him a cowboy hat and a golf shirt, which was supposed to be from Lucas. Then they spent a lot of time driving a borrowed golf cart.

The first day at school, Howie wore his golf shirt and cowboy hat. On his way there, two eighth graders stopped him on the corner of Cholla and Sixty-eighth. The eighth graders took his hat and stepped on it and called him names. Then Howie went home and watched TV shows about doctors and presidents of corporations and women who owned boutiques; he ironed parts of his hat, to fix the creases, and used bleach to get the dirt out. The bleach made parts of the hat white and splotchy. He hung the hat up in his closet, to dry, and when Mrs. Bently came home, she asked him to put away the ironing board. Then she called the school to explain his absence.

Now at school, Mrs. Zuniga, his teacher, gives him lots of books to read and sends him to the library during Reading; apparently, it is too late in the semester for Howie to join a group. The Bluebirds are the smartest, and all girls, but Mrs. Zuniga says he is too far ahead of his class, anyway. Actually, he should be in the next grade. She is going to have to have a talk with Mrs. Bently and the principal, and in the library, Howie sits next to a short girl with a crew cut. Sometimes she punches him in the arm, and sometimes she ignores him.

"I'm new," she says to him one day. "What's your name?"

"Howie."

"Do you like to read?"

"It's okay."

"Do you like to play baseball?"

"Sure," Howie says. He looks up at the librarian, who is frowning. His mother is a librarian, too; he thinks this lady should be nice to him. He says, "I play lots of baseball."

Actually Lucas plays baseball; Howie, hockey. This way, they don't have to compete. But now they both just swing golf clubs, because Lucas is too tired to walk around all the holes, and there is no ice nearby to skate on. Howie says, feeling the muscle in his arm, "Actually, I like golf."

"Your brother has cancer, doesn't he?"

"He's okay. They're going to give him a narrow bone transplant."

The girl punches him in the arm again and says, "Does that hurt?"

"No."

"My name's Melanie," she says, rolling up her sleeve. Now she flexes her arm and says, "Go ahead. Punch me back."

After he punches her back, the librarian takes him by the neck. She lifts him up from his chair and says, "You. To the office."

Now, at night, with Lucas in his hospital bed in downtown Phoenix, Howie has his choice of two bunks. And sometimes Howie thinks Melanie could be his girlfriend, if he liked girls. Lucas likes girls. In Wisconsin, before he got sick, Lucas would talk to them on the phone for hours, especially Lynda Fritag. Lucas said Lynda Fritag wasn't *easy*. Sometimes, when Howie used to be difficult, Mr. Bently practiced on the rowing machine, and Mrs. Bently spent a lot of time explaining things. But Howie hasn't been difficult since they moved to Arizona, and when he punched Melanie in the arm, in the library, she didn't flinch. He knew that she could punch him harder; her arm was hard and had a muscle. The principal was too busy to see Howie, so Howie spoke with his secretary instead. She was a nice lady and asked him if he'd like to go to the nurse. The nurse gave him an empty bed to lie on so he could read all by himself. And at home, lying awake, switching from one bunk to another, Howie tells himself someday he'll fall asleep. Sometimes he hears his mother, crying, and then he puts his hand on his wrist, or his thumb, and tries very hard to hold his breath.

4.

Mr. Bently spends a lot of time rowing in the backyard. Sometimes, he goes a couple miles. Once, before they moved, he and Howie had a conversation. A donor, Mr. Bently explained, is somebody who gives you something, but it's not enough merely to give. You also have to receive. Then Mr. Bently explained why they were going to move to Phoenix; he said it was going to be a new life. There were cactus, he said. And maybe they could have a swimming pool. He said, spreading out his arms, "The Wild West. We'll be cowboys!"

"Can we get a pony?"

Of course pets weren't allowed, at least not until Lucas could take his mask off. Then they'd have to start out small, maybe a new family hamster, or a very short dog. In the meantime, the doctors had to find Lucas someone who was *compatible*.

This weekend, Lucas is home to visit. He sits on the La-Z-Boy by all the boxes still unpacked. He is covered in a blanket to keep the bones from showing. Mrs. Bently carried him into the house without breathing hard. Howie carried in the golf clubs. Then Mrs. Bently asked Lucas if he'd like some ice cream. Maybe he wanted to watch some TV with Howie?

They sat for a while watching TV, but Lucas didn't like to have the sound on. It hurt his head, he said. Sometimes he moaned, and sometimes he started crying. He didn't have any hair anymore and wore a hat so people wouldn't notice. Sometimes, Howie helped Mrs. Bently fix Lucas Kool-Aid, grape or cherry, and Lucas would drink a little before he threw it all up in the pan beside the chair. He was supposed to brush his teeth, after, but all his teeth were falling out, so he didn't bother anymore. Sometimes Howie held the pan closer, so Lucas wouldn't have to reach, but it was hard not to breathe in the smell.

"This is the give part," Howie said.

"Shut up."

Later that night, after his parents are asleep, Howie can't sleep all by himself. He misses the noises his brother used to make, too. Now there is only the noise Howie makes breathing, and he can't hear that if he's breathing; sometimes he rolls in bed and rearranges all the covers. Now he climbs out of bed, trying not to hide, and steps into the living room. Lucas is sitting in the chair wide awake. You can see him by the light of the TV, which is on, and almost blue. He is staring at the stucco on the ceiling, and Howie says, tugging on his pajamas, "Lucas?"

"What."

"You awake?"

"No."

"Can I watch? I mean the dirty parts. I won't tell Mom."

Lucas slides over in his huge chair. He looks at the arm and says, "Don't tell Mom."

"I said I wouldn't."

Later, Howie fixes popcorn in the microwave, and Lucas tries to eat the fluffy ones. Looking up on the screen, there is a woman with breasts bigger than their mother's. They are tan, too, because the woman lives in Florida or California. Howie says, looking up, "Look at those hooters."

"Tits," Lucas says, coughing. "You're supposed to call them tits."

"Boobs," Howie says. "I know."

"Honkers," says Lucas. "Jugs!"

"You're telling me," Howie says, nodding.

5.

Tonight is bathtub night, and Howie's not allowed to lock the door. He sits in the tub, driving his Navy boats. His father went to Inchon and has a gun. Lucas found it in Wisconsin. At first, they were both afraid to touch it, and then when Lucas became sick their parents put the gun someplace else, in order to prevent *accidents.* When the moving van brought their things to their new house, the big furniture came in first. The movers were big and old and wore t-shirts that had been bleached a lot. When they sweated, they smelled like laundry. Mrs. Bently said they lived inside the *shelter* and not to give them any money. Inside the van was Mr. Bently's sports car, and the dressers, and all the shelves for Mrs. Bently's books. One of the rails on Howie's sled had been crushed by the piano, and his father threw the sled into the trash.

"I'll fix it," Howie said. "With my tools."

"It's ruined, Howie. The wood is split." Then Mr. Bently yelled at two men to be careful with Mrs. Bently's couch. He said, looking inside the enormous van, "We'll find you a new one."

In general, Howie knows that when wood splits, you can still use glue and clamps to fix it. Lucas is going to have surgery next week, and everybody is going to go visit. Even a couple friends of his from Milwaukee, just to say hello—a boy named Roger, who is tall and smokes a lot of pot, and also Lynda Fritag, who is very difficult. Sometimes, Howie uses an old baseball bat in the backyard to practice his golf swing. Mrs. Bently says he still has several lessons left. They are already paid for. Maybe he could find a friend?

Now she knocks at the door, to show *courtesy,* before stepping inside the bathroom. She says to Howie, "Did you wash your submarine?"

"Uh huh."

"Your ears?"

He thinks about saying *yes*, but decides he's not supposed to lie. "Not hard," he says, shrugging.

Mrs. Bently kneels by the tub and reaches for a washcloth. She scrubs behind Howie's ears and says, "Howie?"

"Yes."

"Lucas is very sick."

"I know. He needs a donor."

"Your father, he loves you very much. Just because you're not sick doesn't mean that we don't love you."

"I know." Howie shakes the water from his hair. He sets his boats in the basket and says, "He can't receive anymore. Lucas. That's why he has to be transplanted."

When he stands, the water dripping into the bath, Mrs. Bently wraps him in the big blue towel. She lifts him from the water and sets him on his own two feet.

6.

"You're starting to grow," his mother said.

Lucas and Howie also have secrets. Once, when Mr. and Mrs. Bently went out to dinner, Lucas taught himself to drive Mrs. Bently's station wagon in the backyard. In Wisconsin, they had a huge backyard, but you could still see all the tire marks the next day. Also, the bird feeder had been knocked down; the wood, Lucas said, had been split. They used a lot of glue to try and fix it. And Lucas knows that Howie broke the window in their father's den and that Howie steals money from their mother's purse. Before, Lucas would have already beat him to it, so there would be only nickels and dimes left behind. The quarters all went to Lucas first. Lucas also explained to Howie the way sex works. Where you put it, for example. And what the girl's supposed to do next. And all about protection. Lucas said that's what he wants most from the Make-A-Wish Foundation, because Lynda Fritag is also *frigid*. Only now he says it's too late, anyway.

On Howie's birthday, right after he turned eleven, he and Lucas went out onto the golf course. They had about a thousand golf balls, and they had spent a lot of time cleaning them up inside the bathtub. At first they thought they might get a reward. The golf cart was powered by a battery, which meant it didn't use any gasoline, which meant Lucas could drive it if they didn't hit anything and nobody found out. They drove for hours until the battery finally wore out, in a sand trap, near the fifteenth hole. An old man in orange pants started yelling at them, and they had to run away. Lucas couldn't run very fast. He kept falling and they had to throw the suitcase into a pond, where it sank, and then Lucas fainted behind the clubhouse. Howie took off his brother's mask. He hit Lucas on the chest, like a doctor, and eventually Lucas woke up coughing. That night at dinner, before Mr. Bently started taking pictures, Lucas told their parents he felt fine, and Howie knows that lying is what you are not supposed to do, even if you steal money from your mother's purse, or crash her car into the bird feeder. Except for once, Howie hasn't done anything wrong since they've moved to Arizona, but still he often feels bad.

Today at school, during lunch, he is peeing in the Men's when he sees a group of eighth graders coming through the door. If Lucas were here, instead of dying in the hospital, the eighth graders wouldn't pay Howie any mind. Instead, Howie has recently learned, the eighth graders are wrestlers, which means nobody is allowed to get in their way. Otherwise, they give you swirlies.

Howie shakes, fast, and zips. The eighth graders are staring at him now, because he's screaming. He's holding himself with both hands, and bleeding, hopping all over the bathroom screaming.

"Hey," says one of the eighth graders. "Hey, Cowboy,"

and now the eighth grader is trying to be helpful, and Howie is screaming. He's screaming and bleeding because he's hit something big. Finally, he stops leaping. He stands very still, looking down; there at the shank, you can see where the teeth have deliberately caught the flesh. He grips the zipper with his thumb and several fingers, takes a sharp breath, and twists himself free.

"Jesus," says an eighth grader. "Jesus, Cowboy. You gotta go to the nurse."

Instead, Howie grabs a wad of paper towels and shoves them down inside his pants. The blood is hot and sticky, beginning to drip. He reaches for more towels and rushes out of the bathroom for his class. In the classroom, he is in his seat before anybody else. A few minutes later, the nurse steps inside and nods briefly to his teacher, Mrs. Zuniga, who has been writing paragraphs on the blackboard. Howie is sitting in his seat, preparing to do his paragraphs, crying silently, when the nurse steps up behind his desk and rests her hand on his arm. Now, when he stands, the blood dripping into his socks, the room turns still as dust.

7.

Mrs. Zuniga is about sixty-five years old. Maybe eighty. Howie thinks she must be a dud, and on the refrigerator is a photograph taken the day of Howie's birthday. He is standing in front of the Superstition Mountains with his brother, Lucas. Lucas is wearing his mask, and Howie has his new hat, which now hangs neatly inside the closet beside his brother's Christmas presents, which are already wrapped. The closet is huge and still has room for lots of things.

At school, people stop talking when he walks by. He walks with a slight limp, and he is not permitted to take PE for two more weeks. The stitches, all three, are going to take a while to heal, and it causes the most pain when Howie runs too fast, or is sitting still. On his way to school, he now has to walk three extra blocks in order to avoid the wrestlers who saw the whole thing happen.

"Cut his little dick off," one said. "Jesus!"

But Howie knows he didn't cut it off. That's why it hurts so bad. Only Melanie at school talks to him. They sit together in the library and read books silently side by side. Sometimes, she punches him in the arm.

One day Howie says, "Do you like golf?"

"No."

He looks at his book, which has big print, for dumb readers. He reads a sentence. Then he reads it again. The book is all about Kit Carson and how he tamed the West and killed a lot of Indians, and Howie says, "Want to take a lesson with me?"

"Golf?"

"I have lots of friends," Howie says. "Only they don't like golf."

8.

Mr. Bently says there are wild animals, and there are tame animals. Wild animals are the kind you keep outside and don't have to pay attention to. Tame animals, like hamsters, require responsible behavior and processed food. Otherwise they get lost and die. The secret to raising pets is *protection,* Mr. Bently says. If we get a hamster, we have to make sure we have a strong cage. Mr. Bently says, clearing his throat, "Howie, you will have to look after the family hamster all by yourself."

Nobody says a word. Howie is squeezing his legs together, trying to figure out which part still hurts. He reaches for the applesauce.

"Is that acceptable to you, Howie?"

"Uh huh."

For supper, Mrs. Bently cooked frozen enchiladas in the microwave with corn niblets. The applesauce was Mr. Bently's idea. Nobody has remembered to turn on the kitchen light, and the room is growing dark, even if the windows are wide open.

Mrs. Bently says, "Howie wants a pony, Bob. Not a hamster."

"Have to start small," Mr. Bently says. "Maybe next year. Maybe next year, after he's more tall."

"Is it okay," Howie says, "if we *don't* get a hamster. I mean, at least for this year?"

After supper, he helps his mother clear the plates. He listens to the television, which his father is watching all by himself. There is an important baseball game, and during commercials, Mr. Bently hits the Mute. In the kitchen, helping his mother do the dishes, Howie watches her drop a glass into the sink. The glass doesn't break, but it makes a loud noise, and Mr. Bently calls, "What?"

9.

By now Mr. Bently is up to seven miles: each and every night, you can hear him in the backyard, rowing for a couple hours. At the airport, Roger smiles nicely. Roger is a tall boy with acne and a huge duffel bag. Then they wait a long time in order to greet Lynda Fritag who had to take a different airplane. Lynda Fritag has a small carry-on and her purse and a plant for Lucas. Mrs. Bently says the plant is lovely.

At the hospital, Howie spends a lot of time outside on the lawn. While Roger and Lynda visit, Mrs. Bently goes inside the chapel to talk to God, and the minister, who is always friendly. After a couple hours, Lynda and Roger step outside the huge automatic doors, holding hands. Lynda is crying, because it's so sad, the way Lucas is sick, and Roger says, "Maybe we should bring him a pizza?"

At home that night, they eat pizza. Howie picks off the mushrooms and asks Roger questions about wrestling.

"Do you win a lot?" Howie asks.

"Well," Roger says, "I like football. But I have friends who wrestle."

"Do they win a lot?"

"Oh sure," Roger says.

Lynda Fritag says, "Wrestling is disgusting."

"Do you play football?" Howie asks.

"Not really," Roger says. "I mean I'm not on the team or anything."

That night Howie sleeps alone, though according to Mr. Bently, Roger is supposed to be bunking in with him. Lynda Fritag gets the couch. After a while, Howie gets up, and goes into the TV room. Lynda Fritag is lying on the couch with her shirt off. Her bra is unhooked, in back, and Roger is kissing her all over the place.

When she hears him, Lynda sits up fast and tries to find her clothes. She covers her chest with Roger's pants and says, "What do you want?"

"I heard noises," Howie says. "I thought you were watching TV."

"You have to go to school," Roger says. "You're not allowed to be awake."

"It's okay," Howie says. "I just want a drink of water."

That night, when Roger finally comes to bed, he climbs onto the top bunk. Howie thinks most people are supposed to be asleep, though of course lots of people are still awake. Howie is still awake. Roger is still awake. In the hospital, Lucas is probably still awake. Then Roger starts making noises, the kind which make the bed shake. There are springs, squeaking, just the way it was before, and after a while Howie shuts his eyes. He listens to the springs, and to the covers, sliding back and forth, and knows someday it's going to stop.

10.

At the Golden Hills Country Club, sitting in the sand trap, Howie tells Melanie that Roger stole his brother's girlfriend. They are sitting in the sand trap drawing pictures with their tees. Melanie is wearing a pair of blue shorts, which is Howie's favorite color. Also Chip's, which Howie knows, because Chip already said so. Then Chip said, after showing them the door, and pointing his finger, "Play golf."

Howie says, drawing in the sand, "They went to Homecoming together, last year. Before he got sick, and now Lynda doesn't love him anymore."

"How do you know?" Melanie asks.

"I watch about it on TV," Howie says. "First, the girl loves the guy. Then the guy goes away, or falls in love with another girl, and then the girl falls in love with his best friend and makes a lot of phone calls."

"Is Lucas mad?" Melanie asks.

"No," Howie says. "You have to lie a lot too. You have to pretend that everything is the same."

"Oh," Melanie says.

Across the fairway, Howie sees a small pond. Usually the ponds are full of thick green water and have cement. He's not sure if that's precisely where they put the suitcase.

"I'm not old enough to be a donor," he says. "I have to go to school."

"Okay," Melanie says. Now she picks up Howie's hand. She puts his hand in the center of her lap and wraps her fingers all around it.

"Okay," Howie says.

"We're moving," Melanie says. "Next week. But we can still be friends, can't we?"

"I guess so."

Melanie says, giving back his hand, "Does it still hurt?"

It scares him, her hand, touching him. It doesn't hurt at

all, which is the funny part, because normally it does. Even with the stitches all dissolved, it hasn't gone away, and he thinks this is something he will have to tell Lucas. The way Melanie put her hand there. He thinks Lucas will know exactly what he's supposed to do.

11.

The night before the big day, the *operation,* Mr. Bently drives Roger and Lynda Fritag to the airport, while Howie tags along. Actually, his mother and father have had an argument over who is supposed to drive. Actually, Mrs. Bently doesn't want to go anywhere at all; she says the visit was a bad idea. She says Lucas is *depressed.* She says she should have known better and that she's going to spend the night.

On the way to the airport, Howie sits in the back seat with all the luggage. Mostly he is thinking about Melanie, and maybe asking her if she wants to be his girlfriend. At least until she moves away. When Melanie moves away, they won't talk to each other anymore. Howie wonders how long it will take for her to fall in love with somebody like Roger. Not that he is in love with Melanie. Mostly, Howie just likes the way her hair smells, and the way her teeth are so big. He thinks maybe they will be able to move away by then, too, maybe to the same city. He thinks he is going to have to ask her for her phone number. Later, while waiting in traffic, Mr. Bently asks Roger questions about his science project, just to be polite.

In the airport, waiting for all the people to go away, Lynda Fritag says to Mr. Bently, "Thank you, Mr. Bently."

"Thank you, Lynda. It meant a lot to Lucas."

"Bye," says Roger.

"Bye," says Lynda. "We had a great time!"

In the car, on the way back to the hospital, Mr. Bently begins to slap himself. He slaps himself hard, driving, and starts to cry, which makes him sound as if he's going to be sick. After a while Howie rolls down the window and looks into the sky for airplanes. The sky, he knows, is dark, and it's hard to see things in it that don't have any lights.

12.

The day after the funeral for his brother, Lucas Bently, Howie returns to school, where Mrs. Zuniga asks him if he'd like to go to the nurse. Then she asks him if he'd like to go to the library.

On the second day, Mrs. Zuniga gives Howie a pile of letters, each of which was written to him while he was in the library. The letters are from his classmates, all explaining how sad they are for Howie. Sometimes, there are pictures too, and later, after several weeks have passed, during *Show or Tell,* Mrs. Zuniga calls on Howie for the very first time.

He is supposed to describe an important day in his life without any pictures—*Tell,* she says. And Howie knows this isn't the way it's done in Wisconsin. Howie says, standing in front of his class, that the most important day he ever had was when he turned eleven—the day he spent collecting golf balls with his brother, Lucas. And he was going to tell that after they had a couple hundred, they planned to take them to the Pro Club, to give back all the lost balls they found. They thought maybe they might get themselves a big reward. Instead, a woman yelled at them for being stupid. In the back, they could see Chip, drinking beer, and laughing, and the woman said the balls were supposed to be on the range so that the ball man could pick them up with his tractor. The golf balls were not lost. There would be no reward.

But that's not the part Howie told. Lucas always said you're not supposed to tell, and Howie didn't explain the way he never got to drive the cart, but Lucas did, because Lucas said they were just borrowing it. They drove the cart from tee to tee, lobbing golf balls from the suitcase, pretending they were hand grenades. Lucas drove the cart fast as it would go, and Howie had his new hat, which he didn't like to wear anymore because other people took it, and then he did not explain the way the battery died because of all the sand inside the sand trap and the way they had to run away from an old man in orange pants. They had to lie about the suitcase, which was still somewhere in the middle of a pond, and standing in front of his class, Howie realized he wasn't explaining anything at all. Because he couldn't remember any of the things he was allowed to tell.

When you do something wrong, it always makes you feel bad, even if you know you've done it. In the bathroom, scrubbing golf balls, Lucas had taken off his mask. Then Lucas had said, "Don't tell Mom."

"Okay."

"It's a secret," Lucas said. "No one will ever find out."

Lucas meant the way he kept falling down and fainting. He meant Howie was supposed to keep it secret—the kind you never talk about but always carry with you, like a spare quarter to use the phone. Like Lynda Fritag, and the way she looked sitting on the couch with the television on, her skin pale and sweaty. Or the way your father stopped rowing and never came out of the bedroom anymore to go to work.

Afterwards, in front of the entire class, Mrs. Zuniga said, "Howie? Howie, do you have anything more to tell?"

"You're not supposed to take away things that don't belong to you."

"Yes, Howie. That's correct."

"So we gave them back. The golf balls. After we cleaned them."

And Mrs. Zuniga said, smiling, nodding to the class, "Then what?"

"It's secret," Howie said. "I promised to protect it."

Acknowledgments

These stories first appeared in the following publications:

"Light Rock" in *Boulevard*
"Quick" in *Crazyhorse*
"Muscle (And the Possibility of Grace)" in *Denver Quarterly*
"Radical" in the *Gettysburg Review*
"The Last Year of the Soapbox" in the *Hudson Review*
"Horses" in the *Iowa Review*
"All We Shall" in the *Louisville Review*
"The Dark Part" in the *Mid-American Review*
"Wonderland" in *New Letters*
"Insomnia" in *Ploughshares*
"To Comfort" in the *Southern Review*
"Recovery" in *Witness.*

Seven of these stories also appeared in a short story collection published in Germany—*Wonderland,* translated by Christoph Schuenke (Volk und Welt, 1996; Rowohlt, 1998).

I am grateful to those who helped me to make this book, then and now. And to Joy Harris, then and now.
     —T. M. McN.